"Are you serious? You will actually be a pretend best man at the wedding of a person you do not know for me?"

Shut up, Charlie! Just say thank you, then maybe have him swear a blood pact.

By then Beau had pushed his chair back and also stood. He tossed his napkin to the table and said, "It seems so."

Charlie felt as if a pair of hands grabbed her by the waist, lifted her from her chair and propelled her around the table then, for suddenly she was leaning over Beau, flinging her arms around his neck and hugging the life out of him.

Her body a comma curled into his. The heat of him burning through her clothes, till his heart beat in syncopation with her own.

Her inner monologue cleared its throat, waking her from the heady fog. And she pulled away, pushed more like. Once clear, she tugged at her T-shirt and attempted a smile.

"Thank you," she managed. "I mean it, Beau. This will be life-changing."

In a good way for once, she hoped with all her might.

Dear Reader,

Once upon a time, I shared a meme about a girls' weekend that was less about cocktails and hijinks and more about snacking, napping and, most of all, reading. All weekend long. When a friend perked up with "I have the perfect place," we decided, very quickly, that we were really doing this. Needless to say, the excitement factor was off the scale.

We chose a date, packed snuggly clothes and books galore, then set off to stay at her father's then-empty house—a gorgeous craftsman-built home in the scenic Sunshine Coast hinterland.

The weekend was even better than you might imagine. The local towns—in which we breakfasted before going back to our reading—were quaint, artisanal, poetic, gentle and utterly beautiful. The house—situated on a verdant hilltop and overlooking undulating forest with the Pacific beyond—was an absolute dream. Blissed out on reading-inspired dopamine, how could I not choose to set a book in such a place?

Liberties were taken for the sake of the story when it came to the house, local characters and nearby towns, etc. But that view? I didn't change a single thing.

Love,

Ally xxx

ALWAYS THE BRIDESMAID

ALLY BLAKE

Harlequin
ROMANCE

Harlequin®
ROMANCE

ISBN-13: 978-1-335-21612-0

Always the Bridesmaid

Recycling programs for this product may not exist in your area.

 Harlequin Enterprises ULC
22 Adelaide St. West, 41st Floor
Toronto, Ontario M5H 4E3, Canada
www.Harlequin.com

Printed in U.S.A.

Australian author **Ally Blake** loves reading and strong coffee, porch swings and dappled sunshine, beautiful notebooks and soft, dark pencils. Her inquisitive, rambunctious, spectacular children are her exquisite delights. And she adores writing love stories so much she'd write them even if nobody else read them. No wonder, then, having sold over four million copies of her romance novels worldwide, Ally is living her bliss. Find out more about Ally's books at allyblake.com.

Books by Ally Blake

Harlequin Romance

Billion-Dollar Bachelors

Whirlwind Fling to Baby Bombshell
Fake Engagement with the Billionaire
Cinderella Assistant to Boss's Bride

One Year to Wed

Secretly Married to a Prince

Hired by the Mysterious Millionaire
A Week with the Best Man
Crazy About Her Impossible Boss
Brooding Rebel to Baby Daddy
Dream Vacation, Surprise Baby
The Millionaire's Melbourne Proposal
The Wedding Favor

Visit the Author Profile page
at Harlequin.com for more titles.

This book is dedicated to Sharon, who, when I shared a meme about a girls' weekend away during which you do nothing but go to your separate corners and read, said, "And we are doing this when?"

CHAPTER ONE

CHARLOTTE GOODE STOOD in the shade of a pale pink castle-shaped wedding cake the size of a dolls' house. While the bride, Leesa, not two metres away, gawped back at her, eyes glassy, mouth wide with shock.

No wonder, for the bride's eye-wateringly expensive dress, with its vintage lace bodice, and voluminous layers of imported French tulle, was dripping in great globs of rich, gooey mud-brown cake and pale pink buttercream frosting.

The remains of which were stuck to the nooks and crannies of Charlotte's fiercely clenched hand.

For mere moments earlier, Charlotte had shoved her hand deep into the guts of that fairytale cake and grabbed a hearty fistful—in much the same way the bad guy in Indiana Jones and the Temple of Doom *had reached into that guy's chest and come out with his bloody beating heart—before hoicking back her hand and letting the cake fly...*

* * *

Charlie shuddered, attempting to rid herself of the shocking memory.

It had been two years since that fateful day. Her Momentary Lapse of Reason, she called it; to everyone else it had become #cakegate.

Two years since Charlie had stepped into her infamous era. Whether it was the optics of such a manifestly opulent wedding, the fact that Leesa, the bride, was the daughter of a US senator who'd gone apoplectic in the aftermath, or that one perfect photo of the aftermath, their perfectly meme-able faces in twin shocked expressions, for a minute *#cakegate* had trended higher than *#distractedboyfriend* and *#todayyearsold*.

Whatever one called it, she'd become a laughingstock, poison, and unemployable. The life she'd worked, and tried, and hustled so hard to build had ended up in pieces at her well-shod feet.

She looked at her feet now—lifting them from the armrest of the lumpy couch on which she lay, and giving them a wriggle, before ducking the chipped black evidence of a hasty home pedicure back out of sight.

She puffed out a breath, and tried, for the thousandth time, to think of some way she might have fixed things.

What if she'd not been so hasty as to resign from her role as junior event coordinator at the iconic San Francisco Bay Library? What if she'd refused to agree to their demand that she not contact the bride to apologise? What if she explained that she'd had a really good reason why she'd done what she did. That she'd been aiming for the groom, and missed.

Charlie groaned, and squeezed her eyes shut tighter, knowing it wouldn't have helped. For despite all that, she'd done something rash, and unconscionable. And in the end she'd only had herself to blame.

Hence the fact she was scrolling cat videos and nibbling at the bowl of stale mixed nuts balanced precariously on her chest while slouched back on the lumpy cane couch in her parents' sunroom in a house on picturesque hilltop Myrtle Way, in the Sunshine Coast hinterland.

There, *that* ought to distract her from #cakegate. The fact that after leaving home and vowing never to return, she was back living in her parents' place.

Her parents' place.

Charlie kept calling it that even though in actual fact the place had been vacant for years; the captured-in-time furniture, peeling wallpaper, funny smell in the laundry, and overgrown front garden were proof of that.

For when her father had died a number of years back, leaving behind a large collection of jackets with elbow patches and Charlie's habit of looking over her shoulder in case he was still there shaking his head at her in grave disappointment, her mum had hightailed it to the UK the day after she'd buried him. Like a rubber band stretched to its limits that had finally snapped.

"Are you sure?" Charlie's mum had said over the phone when Charlie had managed to track her down in the wilds of Scotland, where she was living these days, to make the mortifying "is it okay if I crash at home for a bit?" call. Her memories of the years spent in that house as snarled as Charlie's own.

After giving her mum the shiniest possible version of becoming an unemployable punch line, Charlie had said, "You know I'd not ask if I had any other choice—"

"Of course, honey," her mother had cooed. "Warning, I have no clue what condition the place is in after all this time. There's nothing owing on the place, the one good thing I can say about your father, but there may be a smidge of land tax due, and a few things that need fixing to make it habitable. But stay. Or sell the thing, and come on over here. There's no room in the caravan, but you'd love Edinburgh. Or, do as I planned, and let the earth eat it alive. Heck, burn it to the ground if that's what you want!"

What pleased Charlie was to take advantage of rent-free shelter, while curling up in a ball till she stopped feeling sorry for herself. Turned out that didn't happen overnight. For living in a falling down, debt-ridden house that she'd vowed never to set foot in again wasn't all it was cracked up to be.

So, she'd shaken herself off, stripped the bed, organised power and water like a proper grown-up, made a deal with the council to pay the eye-watering back taxes bit by bit, and started over. Again.

For Charlie was nothing if not resilient. She'd been knocked down—and, far more importantly, gotten back up again—more times than she could remember.

Only this time it had taken her rather a lot longer than usual to dust herself off. She was hopeful it was proportionate to the event, and not some indication that there was a finite number of times a person could get knocked down before it became just too hard to get back up again.

Then, like some portent of doom, Charlie flinched as an *actual* knock came at the front door.

She squinted up the hall, through the dust motes glittering in a beam of afternoon sunlight.

Eighteen months she'd been there now, and nobody had knocked. Likely because it meant braving the wildly overgrown front drive. There was also the fact she'd not exactly done much in the way of friend-making since she'd come home. Why bother, when she wasn't planning on sticking around. She just needed something—a spark, a sign, a kick in the pants—and she'd be back. Fierce and fighting fit. Till then, scrolling funny cat videos held great appeal.

Another knock. This one a little louder.

It was probably someone selling solar panel plans. Or maybe a tradesperson letting her know her hot water might be cut off for a few days, as yet another house along the street had been knocked down to make way for some contemporary hilltop mega-palace.

For the place on Myrtle Way, for all its drawbacks—distance to the nearest big city, inconsistent Wi-Fi, back steps held together with termite poop—was situated in the prettiest place on the planet.

The road itself wound along the peak of a band of verdant hills, leading to a number of small but popular tourist towns filled with quaint shops and even quainter people. But it was the view east that was the real money shot—a bright blue dome of a sky above layers of rich layers of green undulating forest rolling toward the deep blue distant twinkle of the Pacific beyond.

The gentrification of the area since she'd left was unsurprising. The speed at which it had was enough to give a person whiplash.

Another knock.

Wow, they were *really* keen. Their stickability was next level. It reminded her of…

Heat rushed up Charlie's neck and her belly felt all pins and needly as the aftermath of #cakegate came swimming at her all over again. In the weeks that followed she'd had to battle emails, phone calls, people stopping her on the street to take selfies. And once her address was out there, knocks at her door at any hour.

The breaking point had been an interview with a potential employer, smiling at her as if he'd met her somewhere before. Until something clicked, his eyes widening as he realised who she was. What she'd done. His disappointment had felt like a knife through the heart.

Thank everything good and holy this place was backwater enough that the whiff of #cakegate hadn't followed. But if it found her again, she honestly had no clue what she might do.

Knock. *Knock. Knock-knock-knock.*

Enough was enough.

Cursing the gods of mischief and mayhem who seemed to have taken a liking to her from birth, Charlie tossed her phone to the couch, pushed herself to standing, and padded up the hallway to the door.

A quick check of her T-shirt sporting the mean old guys on *The Muppets* told her she had put on a bra that morning. The messy bun atop her head, and the fact she likely smelled like coffee and a medium to low current level of self-care were what they were.

Then, with a fortifying breath, she whipped open her front door.

To find a man mountain blocking the sun on her wide front veranda.

Even facing away, looking up the curving driveway past the overgrowth, toward the hidden road beyond, it was clear the guy was no door-to-door salesperson. Or a tradie for that matter. Too well-dressed in his slick brown boots, dark jeans, and peacoat a smidge too warm for the subtropical climate.

Too tall, too. Was that a thing? Could a person be too tall to take on a door-to-door job? For the man was mighty at well over six and a half feet and built to match.

Even his hair was a lot. Thick, gloriously tousled, the colour of rich dark chocolate. So soft-looking her fingers curled into her palms.

It was the weirdest thing. Her entire body seemed to be in the midst of some kind of chemical reaction. As if it was trying to tell her something. Had she stood up too fast? Been bitten by something on her walk down the hall?

All that in the space of two seconds.

For then the man turned.

Time seemed to slow as sunlight rained over him, dappled and bright, creating a halo of white gold around his spectacular face. Sparks glinted off black-rimmed glasses, shards of golden light picked out a sharp jaw covered in neat stubble, a straight nose, the outline of the most beautifully carved lips curving into a slow smile—

"Charlotte?"

Memories flickered and flashed, tumbling frantically over one another—rope swings, hide-and-seek, shooting-star watch parties. Picking wildflowers to make potions. A secret space in the small dank nook under the back porch of her house to hide in when her father, or his parents, were being particularly…them. A tumbled mess of laughter, daring, tenderness, rebellion, togetherness, confusion, anger, and the deep ache that comes from falling out with a friend—

Charlie rocked on her feet, as if something had reached in and dragged her through a gap in the space-time continuum.

"Beau?" she said, her voice catching.

It was. It was *Beau Griffin*. The boy next door.

Only he was not a boy anymore. For this Beau was a man. A big stunning manly man. With facial hair and bone structure and shoulders she had to move her head to measure.

Beau huffed out a soft laugh, and shook his head. As if he was as surprised to find her in her parents' home as she was to see him on their front veranda. A crease curved in just the one cheek, lines fanning out from the edges of his glasses behind which resided eyes she'd at one time known better than her own. Eyes the colour of peanut butter. Of autumn leaves. She may once have written a *very* secret poem saying as much.

Thankfully, some seed of self-control burst inside her. Which was a small miracle, considering her history of giving into urges that erred on the side of self-destructive.

"Beau!" she said again. Then, "Beau Griffin. It's been *forever.*"

Not quite, though. For she remembered the date, the day, what they were both wearing. The awful fight they'd had the night before. How she'd had to cross her arms so tight across her chest in order to stop the shakes when he'd driven away to take on the phenomenal early scholarship he'd been awarded, and not looked back.

How her father—a "renowned doctor of chemistry" to anyone who asked, as opposed to mildly successful high school science teacher—had moved in behind her, and hissed into her ear, asking why with all the advantages she'd been given—aka being his daughter—*she* couldn't be *more like Beau.*

"It's so good to see you!" she said, feeling *totally* fine about all that now. Then she reached out and gave his arm a chummy smack, and her hand bounced off what felt like wool over solid concrete. *That* was new.

"I thought," he said, brow furrowing over his glasses, "I'd heard you were working overseas?"

And didn't that just set off a swirl of feelings inside her, imagining he must have googled her or secretly stalked her social media at some point.

Then, as if it had been lying in wait, #cakegate

poked out its head. Had he seen the memes? Or heard the song someone had made that had gone viral for a half second, using the gasps and chair scrapes and clanking plates as percussion.

Her whole body felt as if it was curling on itself as she waited for the follow up. The weirdness that always came next. Hell, if she saw *disappointment* in Beau Griffin's eyes she might never recover. But nothing more came of it, and she relaxed a very little.

"Mm-hmm," she said. "I'm crashing here for a little bit. Passing through really. And you? Working hard doing something amazing I bet."

Last she'd heard *he* was in Sydney, fronting a groundbreaking team of engineers working to invent some renewable, green clean energy battery, or engine, or something, that was going to save the world. For yes, she had cyber-stalked him a while back, before she realised it didn't make her feel any better about how things had gone down.

He lifted a hand to the back of his neck, a classic Beau move, giving him the air of a tortured poet. "Busy enough. Though I've just... I'm taking some time off right now."

She might have asked, *Time off from what?* or *Why?* but there was the fact that he was looking at her mouth. Like, *really* looking.

Then his hand lifted from its position hooked into the front of a pair of awfully flattering jeans and both she and her inner monologue had no words as he reached up. His fingers hovered an inch away from her jaw, his thumb hooked as if he might brush her lips. While his gaze was so focused, warmth spread through her like liquid sunshine.

Then, in Beau's voice yet not Beau's voice for it was lower than she remembered, deep, with a husky edge, said, "You have a small flake of something on the corner of your mouth."

Sorry, what now?

Charlie's tongue darted out, catching a *not small* flake of peanut skin that had been stuck there. The entire time.

All the strange warmth that had been dancing through her zoomed straight to her cheeks as she wiped quickly at her mouth, to find it *covered* in peanut salt. Looking down she found yet more salt, *more peanut flakes,* glittering her boobs.

She brushed herself down, frantically flapped her shirt, then started to laugh. Cackling, really, for the first time in what felt like eons. Till her stomach hurt.

"You have no idea how much I needed that," she said, once she was recovered. Then she looked up at him, arms wide, and said, "Truth is, I'm a hot mess. How the heck are you?"

"I'm…fine," he said, as if, despite all evidence to the contrary, he'd needed that moment to be sure. Then, "Surprised to see you. Thrilled, that it was you who opened the door, but surprised."

"Thrilled, you say?"

The crease in his right cheek grew a little deeper, and even while the smile never quite reached his eyes, her knees all but gave way.

"I was beginning to wonder how many more times I should knock before it bordered on too many," Beau said.

Charlie braced a hip on the doorjamb. "Oh, it was definitely too many. I was ready to set the dogs on you."

When he looked over her shoulder, down her parents' front hall, as if expecting a horde of Dobermans to come at him, she added, "Metaphorically," and got another half smile for her efforts.

As an inconvenient bloom rose inside her, Charlie wrapped the old wrap tighter about herself.

"Was there a reason for the knocking?" she asked, rather than the zillion other questions knocking about inside her head.

Why are you here? How have you been? Where have you been? Are you okay? Like, really okay? What happened to us? Are you married? Kids? Do you ever think of me? Of us? Do you ever wonder if the adventures we had before the whole weird "falling out" thing might end up being the best times of our lives?

Something flashed behind his eyes, making her wonder if he, too, was choosing which of a dozen questions to start with, before he went with, "How are your parents? Are they still about?"

Parents. Meaning he must not know about her father. She'd always imagined that while she and Beau had not spoken in years, her father had found a way to stay in contact over the years, for he'd seen Beau as the child he'd believed he deserved. The fact that she'd been wrong about that loosened something inside her.

"Dad passed away a while back," Charlie said. "Mum is travelling the Scottish wilderness in a campervan with her *lover*, Alfredo."

Beau lifted his chin in a nod, as if that all tracked. What he didn't do was offer up any condolences over her father's fate. Which she appreciated. For Beau understood that she'd have struggled to accept it. In fact, he was the only person who ever truly would.

She did him the same courtesy. She'd already moved overseas, having nabbed a green card in the visa lottery, when Beau's parents had died. Her mother had called to tell her—gas inhalation in their kitchen, classified accidental, evidence suggesting both were likely too high to even notice.

His parents. Their house. Oh, no.

Before she could second-guess herself, Charlie leaped out onto the veranda, grabbed Beau's arm, her hand sliding into the crook of his elbow the way it had done a thousand times before, and used the element of surprise to spin him so that their backs were to the place where Beau's childhood home used to be.

For it was one of the most recent to have been torn down. Wrecking balls and bulldozers. The whole nine yards. It had been quite the show.

While it had probably a good thing, considering its macabre history, a gargantuan sharp-edged beast of a structure had begun to be constructed in its place. And while Beau's childhood had been more chaotic than hers, even downright frightening at times, foundational memories could be complicated. She knew.

"Charlotte?" Beau said again, an all too familiar note of indulgence in his voice.

"Mm-hmm?"

"Is there a reason we're looking at your rubbish bins."

"Yep."

Chances were, he knew about the house, right? Though, from the road it looked the same as it always had—big brick pillars covered in moss and wild jasmine, the gate long since gone, long driveway dipping past shrubs and lush trees blocking any view of the house settled into the gently sloping hillside at the rear.

But still he waited. Big to her small. All still stoicism to her constant fidgets. Patience to her restlessness. So warm and strong. So *Beau*.

A deep psychic ache rose up inside her then.

The years she'd missed, even when he'd still been around. Wondering what she'd done to make him pull away, hating not knowing where they had gone so wrong.

So, yeah, maybe *grabbing* the guy hadn't been the best move.

Then Beau made a sound. Or maybe he flexed beneath her gripping hand. Either way she looked up to find his gaze questioning. When his mouth did the quirk thing, the cheek bracket bracketing for all it was worth, she let go as if burned.

And moved away from him, keeping his attention in the bin direction, which was probably what she *ought* to have done in the first place. *Clicked her fingers. Look over here!*

Then she said. "I have to tell you something."

"Okay."

"Your house… Your *parents'* old house—it's no longer there. And now they're building some modern monstrosity in its place. All sooty wood, cantilever architecture, with the charm of a weapons facility. It's as if the new owner has the hots for *Grand Designs* and hopes to blow out their harebrained budget in the name of owning their very own Mojo Dojo Casa House."

Beau's eyebrows slowly rose. Then he turned, as if to see for himself.

In a panic, Charlie grabbed him by both arms this time. Holy hell, the man was made of concrete. "I just—" She stopped to clear her throat. "I didn't want you to head over there, unprepared."

And as he looked at her, once again the memories just flooded on in. She, his great defender. Taking on school bullies, sneaking him food when it was clear he'd gone without, forcing him on adventures to distract him from whatever went on behind his front door that made him look so haunted all the damn time. His friendship giving her quiet assurance that she was worthy of it.

Until the summer she turned sixteen, and their friendship had gone up in smoke.

"May I?" he said, a hand reaching to open his jacket.

Realising she still held him, she let go. Stepping back, she put her hands in the back pockets of her short cut-offs so that she'd not grab the guy again. Sheesh!

Beau reached for his phone, swiped it open and held up a picture of *her* front porch. A strange package thereupon.

Charlie looked around to find no such package. "I don't understand."

"This is why I came knocking. And knocking some more. My builders received this message yesterday saying some bathroom fittings they had been waiting for had been delivered. Only this was the image the delivery company sent as proof. Only it's not my new front porch, it's yours."

His new front porch?

Charlie's gaze swung past his big shoulders to the trees blocking the view of the house next door. "I don't understand. Your house was sold after your parents—"

She bit her lip. According to her mum, debt collectors had swept in and picked it clean before the bank sold it for a pittance. A series of renters had moved in and out before her mother left and any connection to the house next door had been lost.

"I recently repurchased the place," Beau said.

Charlie, moving back into the safety of the doorway, watched him look toward the house next door, the sliver of his face she could see unreadable.

"Recently?" she pressed. "Meaning you bought it…in order to *knock it down*?"

He turned back to her, then. A rueful smile on his face as he said, "I suppose I did."

And again she noted that the smile didn't quite reach his eyes. In the old days that would have been her sign to drag him up a tree so that they could spy on her other neighbour, or under the back porch for a game of speed Uno.

Now she had nothing for him but, "Wow."

"You haven't considered doing the same?" he asked.

"Me? No!" she said, her hand leaping to her heart before she dropped it back to her side. For one thing, what with her situation and back taxes, *she* didn't have the funds to fix the dodgy wiring, or look into the water stains on the ceiling, much less rebuild an entire house.

As to selling up? She *could* do that. Reinvest, move on. Her mother had even given the green light to burn the place to the ground. Yet she, the queen of burning it all down, was holding back on making a decision. Something keeping her put for the minute. And she wasn't quite ready to unpack what that might be.

Beau, on the other hand, appeared totally cool with having razed his childhood home.

Beau, who'd been the sweetest little kid on the planet; the kind who'd step over an ants' nest and never take the first turn. Who, even when he'd begun to make a name for himself, winning every national science championship there was, had hosted online Dungeons and Dragons games from the local library computers, because he was too shy to do so in person. Teen Beau had been more of an enigma, even before things had gone pear-shaped between them.

But he'd always been forgiving. Of her, when she pushed too hard. Of the kids at school who pegged them both as outsiders and treated them as such. Of his parents, despite what they'd put him through.

Clearly, she'd been mistaken.

When she realised they were both just looking at one another again, and her skin began to warm,

Charlie said, "Sorry. I never saw that package in the photo. Maybe check with the delivery guys?"

He blinked as if pulling himself from his own fog of memories, then said, "Will do."

Then, when Beau looked to the driveway, as if making to leave, Charlie found herself saying:

"And who do I call if I want to complain about the week of cold showers I was just forced to endure?"

That time the crinkles most definitely reached his eyes. Happy warmth flooded through her, reminding her how deeply satisfying it had been, all those years ago, to make this guy smile.

"Plumbing is all done," Beau assured her with a tilt of his head, "so any cold showers you take from here should be by choice." And was his voice a little dry? The kind of dry that scraped down a woman's insides leaving a scratchy feeling in its wake. *Her* insides. She was the woman.

"If I get any more mystery packages?" she found herself asking.

After a beat, and a long breath in, Beau said, "Let the builders know."

The builders. Not him.

Charlie swallowed, and nodded. "Sure. Of course." Then she stepped back and reached blindly for the door handle. "I was in the middle of something," aka scrolling cat videos, "and I really should get back to it. It was really nice to see you, Beau. Hope all goes well with the monstrosity!"

Beau's mouth was open when she shut the door.

Charlie spun and leaned against the door, her head falling back to thunk against the wood.

Once she was sure enough the guy wasn't about to knock again, she pushed off the door and tiptoed back down the hall to the sunroom. Where she sat on the lumpy cane couch, grabbed a cushion, hugged it to her chest, and stared into the middle distance.

So that was Beau Griffin. The once upon a time gentle to her wild. The sense to her daring. Twin stars revolving around a near-permanent state of imminent danger, keeping one another from flinging out into the void. All grown up.

What was his plan for the house next door? Was he going to sell it? Rent it out? Or keep it for a vacation home? Surely, he wasn't moving back in. Not that it mattered. Not him, not his house. It was nothing to her.

It was enough to be on the lookout for that one great spark of inspiration that might get her out from under the #cakegate fugue. After which she'd be out of there! Faster than lightning.

She would find some place new. Some place entirely devoid of memories to make her mark. For while life might *try* to knock her down, the memories tripped her every damn time.

CHAPTER TWO

A MINUTE LATER Charlie's phone buzzed.

Her heart stuttered when for a half second she wondered if it might be Beau. Beau who didn't have her number, and who'd made no effort to give her his even after she'd given him the perfect opener.

Rolling her eyes at herself, she pulled herself back to sitting in order to read the messages.

Helloooooo!!! Is this Charlotte Goode???

She read it again—her form of dyslexia meaning she often had to read things multiple times for them to sink in—and counted three exclamation marks *and* three questions marks. Whomever they were, top points for enthusiasm!

When more messages came through, *bing-bing-bing*, she clicked on the text-to-speech mode to speed things up, and listened as the dismembered voice said:

"My name is Annie! Martine Jones gave me

your number! She told me what you did for her, and OMG, she could not have raved more!"

Martine was a recent and pretty decent client. For in her hustle to make money to pay back taxes and you know, eat, she'd kind of accidentally started a fledgling new venture. A hobby, really, that could thankfully pay her bills. She'd been loath to call it anything more than that just yet, for surely that would be baiting the #cakegate gods.

A month after coming home, her mum had called, saying one of Charlie's second cousins, Rosie, who she'd apparently once played under a garden sprinkler naked with as a kid, was getting married. Rosie's maid of honour had broken her nose in a skiing accident, and Charlie's mum had suggested Charlie could fill in.

It had no doubt been her way of getting Charlie out of the house, as if she could sense her continued reticence even from far, far away. Also because Charlie was event-trained and available. Win-win!

For much the same reasons, Charlie had agreed. And whether it was she had no skin in the game, or she'd so needed to do something where she felt useful again, it had been the best fun. Easy. Exciting even, putting out real-time spot fires before they could flare up.

Her cousin could not have been more grateful. While wedding guests, who'd heard the story of all she'd pulled off in so short a time, had asked for her business card in case they could use her in *their* wedding party.

Cousin Rosie—a career counsellor who had not paid her a cent—had leaped in, gushing, "She's worth every penny!" with a conspiratorial wink.

And that's how *Always the Bridesmaid*—Charlie's kind of, accidental, money-maker—had been born.

Her phone buzzed again.

I would love to meet with you, to see if there's a chance that you could squeeze me into what must be an insanely packed schedule.

Brace yourself: there will be three hundred + guests, and it's in six weeks!

You would be literally SAVING MY LIFE!!!

Charlie coughed out a laugh at *insanely packed schedule*. She wished. Only not out loud. No point getting too excited about what it might one day become, for it could all come tumbling down just as quickly.

But it was nice hearing such things in her father's house. In fact, she turned up the volume, lifted her phone and played the next messages, in case a certain ghost might by some chance be listening in.

The way you stopped her nephew from spiking the punch, genius!

The dad jokes you pull out every time she tried on her dress, knowing her dad wouldn't be there.

Forget the numbers and the crunch time. The brilliance of what you do is none of that matters for you'd be all mine! My very own professional bestie!

A professional bestie. She'd never thought of it that way. But if Always the Bridesmaid *was* ever big enough to demand a mission statement that'd be close.

Then the idea of being anyone's bestie only brought up thoughts of Beau Griffin. How tight they'd been, how important to one another. Until they weren't. She'd been too confused back then, too hurt, too sixteen years old to confront him. To ask what it was about her bestie-ness he'd found so easy to live without. But now?

"Argh!" she growled. Then, "You know what? Screw it."

She looked at her calendar to find she was due to meet up with Isla—a client who was fretting about her choice of wedding dress, and needed some cheerleading—the next day.

She texted back, but not before checking her spelling three times.

Free tomorrow morning?

Within a minute a meeting place was booked.

Charlie replied to a few questions from her book-keeper, Julia, via voice notes as she walked up the hill toward the café the next morning. Always the Bridesmaid wasn't exactly big enough to require such help, but Charlie's dyslexia was.

Her condition hadn't been picked up until rather late, around halfway through primary school, as she'd hid it behind being precocious, asking a lot of questions when the words made no sense, being the most helpful. Anything to distract people from thinking she was stupid. Incapable. Lazy.

She got enough of that at home.

Once diagnosed, her mum and teachers had done their best to help her navigate it, but her father blocked them at every chance. *No child of his required learning assistance.*

Only as an adult, in fact the year she'd spent in San Francisco, had she had the means, and the courage, to find her own dyslexia therapist. And it had changed her life. She'd discovered her brand of dyslexia wasn't merely swapping numbers and letters, it was also the likely reason behind her excellent memory, and the fact that reading body language and knowing how much personal space to allow for were not her forte.

The flipside? Give her a problem and she'd find a way to solve it. It was her superpower.

She had been getting a handle on things, and acknowledging that so many of the things she'd struggled with were *not* her fault, when #cakegate happened.

Leaving her therapist had knocked her as much as losing her apartment, her employment, the version of herself she'd worked so hard to become.

When Always the Bridesmaid had become a thing, and she'd found Julia's details in a hobby business forum. After the second, super-long, excited email from Julia, Charlie had braved up, called her and let her know that due to her dyslexia, she just couldn't function that way.

Julia had paused for a beat and said, "How would voice messages go?"

Needless to say, Julia was a blessed relief.

Charlie walked past the Clock Shop, the old windmill, boho cafés, and handmade toy shops, listening again to the dozen messages Annie had sent her that morning. Picking out the highlights:

Three hundred plus guests.

Six weeks.

Money no object.

Taking the final message with a grain of salt, an event that size would still be a step up from the mostly local DIY weddings that Always the Bridesmaid had worked thus far. In fact, it was leaning a *little* close to the kinds of event she had assisted in organising during her San Francisco Library days, but whereas a few months ago it might have brought her out in hives, she felt ready.

In fact, it felt like just the right time.

Hadn't she been waiting for a sign? A spark? A kick in the pants? Then Beau Griffin had turned up on her doorstep, looking all windswept, and solid. Like the ghost of summers past, reminding her of who she used to be—how bolshie, and fierce, how nothing could stop her.

She breathed out in relief as she finally reached the meeting spot—the Pretty Kitty Café. Only to head inside and find…actual cats. Everywhere.

"Hand sanitiser over there," the emo girl on reception intoned, pointing to the other side of a glass partition where the patrons and cats hung out together. "Don't leave your glass unattended as they will knock it over. You can pick up any cat, bar Jerry." She pointed to a picture tacked to the glass wall; a half tiger, half house cat looking menacingly at the camera.

Something beyond the image caught Charlie's eye. She refocused to see a woman in a fluffy pink top, holding a fluffy white kitten, and madly waving her hand.

And all remnants of any chipper feelings Charlie had been harbouring about this meeting fled as dread poured into its place.

For "Annie!!!" turned out to be Anushka Patel.

While Charlie had lost any appetite for celeb

gossip after #cakegate, there was no avoiding Anushka Patel—an ex-reality TV dating show star turned radio drive time cohost, who famously dressed like a Manga character, and had become an actual postfeminist icon after infamously dumping her football star boyfriend for refusing to read *Twilight*.

Three hundred guests Charlie could do.

A wedding in six weeks Charlie could do.

That level of media interest, of public interest, Anushka Patel had shining upon her day and night, simply by existing? No, nope. No way in hell.

When Anushka waved for her to come in, it was either do just that, or spin on her heel and make a run for it. The least she could do, as a professional bestie and all, was meet with the woman, and let her down gently.

"Charlotte!!!" Anushka cried, the triple exclamation marks absolutely implied.

Holding her breath against the cloying scent of kitty litter and flea powder, Charlie narrowly avoided stepping on a kitten as she made her way to the hot pink booth in the corner. "Annie as in Anushka?"

Anushka waved her spare hand at Charlie, glitter seeming to waft from her person, before yanking her into a tight one-armed hug. "I know. Sorry. I never type my real name. Hacking, you know."

"Totally," said Charlie. Though thankfully her moment in the sun had been hot enough to burn, but had burned itself before hacking had become a thing. And she'd really prefer to keep it that way.

Anushka made smoochie noises at the kitten before placing it on the floor at her feet, then sat, and stared at Charlie as if feeding off her energy.

"Gosh, you're pretty," Anushka said in her famously breathy voice. "And I *know* pretty. Most of us on the kinds of shows I've done are 'makeup and good colourist' pretty. But a forties gumshoe detective would give up his career over your peepers."

Charlie blinked eyes she'd always thought made her look a bit like a Disney chipmunk, as she slid into the booth. "I have cellulite, if that helps."

"Oh, that helps a lot."

"Now," said Charlie, when Anushka took in a breath. "Before we go any further——"

"No!" said Anushka, her face downfallen. "Please don't say no. I *need* you. I've felt so much better the past day, since we spoke. Now I can't imagine going ahead without you."

Charlie wondered if Anushka was waving catnip under Charlie's nose. You need me? I'm just that capable?

But no. The risk that someone looking to Anushka's wedding for clickbait would put two and two together was too great. And while risk might *once* have been her middle name, she had to be more careful now. Unsure how many more failures she had in her.

"I'm really sorry," Charlie said, flinching when something furry brushed by her ankle. "My schedule simply won't allow it. But I'd be happy to refer you to my wonderful associate, Julia."

Yep, Julia the bookkeeper. For Julia had agreed to take on the bookkeeping at a vastly reduced fee if she could learn the ropes, so that she might "move up in the organisation." Julia had taken on a couple of clients down Byron Bay way, while Charlie charged a finder's fee for basically doing nothing, and it had gone just fine.

"Julia lives a couple of hours away, but is wonderful," Charlie assured her. "Perky, tough when needed, so organised it's terrifying—"

Anushka held up a finger, then grabbed a pen—glittery, pink, with a pompom on top—and paper—pink with sparkly edges—and said, "I'm sure anyone you recommend would be lovely. But I am a gut person, and my gut tells me I need you. Only you."

Anushka slid the piece of paper across the table, and Charlie's gaze fell upon a figure that made her eyes widen so fast it was miracle her eyelids didn't turn inside out.

"Anushka, I'm not sure what it is you think I do, but for this number you'd be right in requesting unicorns to ride in on, a honeymoon in space, and out-of-season flowers in your bouquet."

A skinny grey cat leaped onto the table, and Anushka lifted her milkshake with practiced adeptness as she said, "I don't want all that. I want you."

Charlie kept looking at the number, her eyes burning from not blinking, in case when she did the number might change.

It was serious money. The kind of money a businesswoman who was aware of what her experience, bravado, and capability were worth might demand.

It hit like a punch to the gut how deliberately she'd been undervaluing herself.

Damn you, #cakegate.

And damn Richard, her ex, the #cakegate groom, the one she'd *tried* to throw a handful of squished cake at, and missed.

She'd not originally been on the roster for that event, but he'd known she worked there. Meaning he could have convinced his wife-to-be to have the reception somewhere else, just in case. But that wasn't Richard's way.

The gods of mischief, and stomach flu, decreed that she be called in at the absolute last minute to take over from a sick colleague once the reception was already underway. She'd been on cake duty, literally watching the thing, making sure no one came too close, when she felt someone move in behind her.

How do you like me now? he'd muttered, his voice filled with caustic pride.

No more than I did when I left you, she'd shot back, her heart thudding in her throat as she'd looked around for someone to take her place.

At which point he'd called her a filthy liar, and a fool, for she would cry herself to sleep that night, realising just how wholly she'd screwed up in letting him go. Then he'd called her a word only one other man had ever called her. And even then he'd only done it once, before he'd kicked her out of her home.

"You've gone terribly serious all of a sudden," said Anushka.

And Charlie snapped back to the present. "You've surprised me, which I'm sure was the point."

Anushka batted her lashes Charlie's way.

"Tell me about your fiancé," Charlie blurted, needing to shake off the shakes that had started in her hands and would soon have her wanting to curl into a ball if she didn't stop them. Besides, if she was truly considering this, best make sure the guy wasn't a serial killer, prank show host, or yet another ex.

In Charlie-land, things that seemed too good to be true usually were.

"Of course!" said Anushka. "I can't believe I

didn't start there. This is Bobby." Then she slid her phone across the table, and leaned her chin on her hand, her expression softening so that Charlie could all but see the cartoon hearts popping over her head.

The photo showed Anushka clinging happily to a man with curly brown hair, deep brown eyes, moustache, nice smile, a tad shorter than she. A bright red race car in the background.

"Your Bobby is *Bobby Kent*?" The rise at the end of Charlie's sentence was due to the fact that while Anushka was a press magnet, Bobby Kent was an absolute superstar. Australia's best ever Indigenous racing car driver, he was even more of a media magnet than his fiancée.

Anushka nodded. "Isn't he adorable?"

Charlie nodded, while thinking she couldn't do this. More to the point, she dared not.

Dammit. Truly. Would #cakegate loom over her forever? Maybe. Maybe her hopes for finding her way to eventually something wonderful were crazy. Maybe she was destined to stay slow and steady, if she wanted to go through life without people looking at her with such—

"Disappointment," said Anushka.

Charlie blinked.

"I mean," Anushka went on, "they've never explicitly made me feel that way, his parents. They just love their son so very much. I want them to feel sure that I am good for him, while also being my true self. And while I honestly do not care what my wedding day looks like, or tastes like, or sounds like, so long as I'm standing by Bobby, it would be helpful to have someone who's unassailably on my side. You know?"

Charlie knew all too well. And she was *good* at it. She always had been, thanks to Beau Griffin. He'd been her patient zero—dragging him into madcap adventures, distracting with speed Uno, making sure he was fed, watered, and supported.

She might have taken the long way around, but when forced to pare back, to do something spare and honest in order to make ends meet, this was what she'd fallen into. Being a professional bestie.

Charlie made to open her mouth to say, "Hell yes!" when Anushka cut her off.

"There's one more thing."

Of course there was.

"That fee," Anushka said nodding toward the sparkly pink note gripped in Charlie's hand. "It covers hiring *you* as my maid of honour, and a *you* for Bobby as well."

"I'm sorry?"

"Bobby's friends are wonderful, but they're all like him—used to being looked after. Bobby needs a good, honest, solid best man who can cut it with the Kents, keep Bobby's friends on the straight and narrow, and work happily under your purview."

A best man?

And there it was—the foot that had been sticking out, ready to trip her this whole time.

She didn't *know* any men in the area. Well, there was Bryan, her clinically shy mechanic. And Phil, the local grocer who was eighty if he was a day. The closest she came on the daily were the builders at Beau's place next door who she sometimes heard chatting and laughing if she kept her front window open. One might have been named Macca?

Beau's place. Beau.

She knew Beau.

No. Don't be ridiculous. For one thing, when she'd given him an opener to keep in touch, he'd totally ghosted her.

Hadn't he said he'd taken some time off? her inner monologue piped up.

Irrelevant, she shot back.

For what did that mean? A week? A day? Chances were he was back in Sydney already, twerking engine nuts, or whatever it was that he did.

Yeah, no. Not a chance.

A chance. That's what this felt like. A second chance. Heck, it was more like her seventh. It was a big one, at the very least. A chance to prove to herself that she could do this. That she deserved a shot, at least.

All she had to do was take on a job she could

do with her eyes closed, stay in the background, and her life might just change.

"Can you give me a day?" she blurted, before she could change her mind.

Anushka bounced gently on her seat, as she suddenly had two new kittens in her arms.

"No promises," said Charlie.

Anushka shook her head. While grinning as if certain it was fait accompli.

A day. A day to do what? Wander the streets of Maleny holding up a Wanted Best Man sign? See if there was an agency from which she could source such a specific person, someone solid she could trust to represent her in what might be the biggest moment in her career thus far?

Someone like Beau.

No! Besides, she had no way to contact Beau even if she wanted him. She *could* pop her head over the rose bushes, and see if any of the builders might give up his number.

No, she didn't want him, just someone like him.

Not that she *wanted* someone like him. She merely had a use for him. Nope, that didn't sound any better, even in her head.

She shook it off, or tried her best. While knowing now she'd thought it, it would burrow its way in. Like one of those frogs that went underground, for years sometimes, waiting for rain, at which point up it would jump ready and raring to breed.

Great, now we'll spend all afternoon imagin-

ing breeding with Beau Griffin, her inner monologue chuffed.

Enough! she shouted inside her own head. *Focus.*

For it wasn't just the money. It was the contacts. Word of mouth was everything in her business. *Her business*. For that's what Always the Bridesmaid was. Not a job. Something she'd created from nothing.

"Now, let me buy you something sickly sweet and pink to celebrate."

Anushka smiled as she waggled her fingers at a passing waiter, and the stress lines Charlie had missed at first glance, now stood out like footprints in wet sand. As if she'd been holding herself together with hope and positivity for so long she was collapsing in on herself.

Charlie didn't need a day.

If Beau had been the ghost of summers past, then Anushka was her ghost of summers present. And if anyone learned anything from *The Muppet Christmas Carol*, it was that those ghosts knew their stuff.

She'd find a best man.

She'd put Always the Bridesmaid on the map.

Just like that, Charlie Goode's moxie was back.

CHAPTER THREE

BEAU GRIFFIN WAS known for being a man prepared.

Existing in a constant state of readiness, having already run every possible scenario in his head—a skill learned during a childhood spent avoiding the Department of Child Services—was a big reason behind his company's rapid success. It had also been the only way to survive growing up in the house on Myrtle Way.

Only now his ability to make even the smallest decisions had up and left. Eggs for breakfast or muesli? The blue shirt or the other blue shirt? More to the point, what did it matter?

Not great timing, considering the passion project he'd been working on his entire life—the Luculent Engine—was going through its most rigorous review yet, and the architecturally challenging house he'd pushed to have built as soon as possible required decisive choices quickly made.

It was the final reason why he'd decided to take time off, to see the build through to its bitter end. The reason he chose to focus on, at least.

"How's it looking?" Matt—Beau's business partner and best friend—asked through the speaker in Beau's watch. Matt who was back in Sydney, holding up the fort, when considering the past few months, it should very much have been the other way around.

"Much the same," said Beau, standing in the backyard just beyond the edge of bomb site that was his old backyard, hands on hips, gaze on the jutting corner of the gargantuan framework leaning ominously over the giant muddy footprint gouged out of the land.

All the personality of a weapons facility came at him in Charlotte Goode's matter of fact way. And despite how strangely disquieting it had been, seeing her again, he found himself huffing out a laugh.

The house, he reminded himself, bringing his attention, unhinged as it was of late, back to where he wished his focus to remain.

And yet Beau's gaze shifted left, to the wall of thorny rose bushes that created a barrier between their two yards. Echoes, shadows flickering gently in the depths of his mind—a grazed knee, a hand reaching from a higher branch, overlapping front teeth in a wide grin, long dark auburn hair peppered with pollen. A secret handshake, complete with spit and dirt under the nails. A safe place to wait out a storm.

He deliberately dragged his gaze back to the house.

Thoughts of Charlotte Goode leaning against her doorjamb looking lush, and insouciant, and hectic could wait. Or better yet, they could quietly go away. For he'd not come back to this place in search of what seeing her had unearthed in him; a visceral reminder of the time before his childhood home had been summarily wiped from the earth.

He'd come back looking for…what? Clarity? Closure? The key to his current unravelling so that he could turn the thing and find his way back? He honestly had no idea.

All he knew was that Matt had lost Milly—the mother of his kids, the right hand to his left—to cancer—several months before and nothing he said or did made sense anymore.

They'd been great friends, the three of them, since they met at university. As Matt and Milly paired off, got married, had kids, their family became Beau's family. Dinners at the coffee table, finger paint on the walls, laughter and quiet luxury and arguments that never went deeper than surface scratches. A family so polar opposite from the one he'd grown up with as to be laughable.

Milly's diagnosis had come out of nowhere, the disease taking her with such ferocity, ravaging her, the woman Beau considered a sister. It had sent Beau into the kind of tailspin Matt hadn't had the luxury of indulging in, considering the two little ones he had to stay strong for.

It could have imploded—his long friendship with Matt, their company Luculent—taking down all they'd built with it. Except they saw how close they came, and they spoke of it, honestly, constantly: Beau's lack of drive, his faltering focus; Matt's loneliness, and fury, and his determination to get his and Milly's kids, Tasha and Drew, through as unharmed by it all as possible.

Till even Matt had had enough, telling Beau to take some time off—get some perspective. Give himself a break. Luculent had been Milly's as much as it had been theirs, and it was at an all-time high—their engine in review, the world itching for more like it, faster, better. The pendulum would only hold on so long before a downward swing.

Beau was told to figure out what he wanted.

He stared up at the house as if it might have the answers.

It loomed greyly over him and gave nothing away.

"Can you see better now, how it might end up?" Matt asked.

Beau could not. Perhaps because when designing the place, his instructions had been simple: *Make it unrecognizable.*

It *should*, he believed, look less imposing once it was painted, clad in all the designer extras that would "soften the exterior" according to his architect. Once the landscaping was complete and the backyard looked less like the psychological cleansing it so clearly was.

"Beau?" Matt's voice called.

Beau came back into his skin only to feel as if it no longer fit right. It had been that way for months now. As if he contained too much blank space, filled with unseeable, unknown feelings, wanting out. Far too close to how his parents had felt before medicating their way to oblivion.

"It'll be big," he said, dragging his eyes back to the edifice.

Matt laughed. "No surprise there. You do nothing by halves, big dog. It's just not in you."

Speaking of big dogs, Beau whistled and Moose bounded out of the brambles that now seemed to fill the gorge at the rear of the property. Ears flapping, tongue lolling, covered in filth, the dog sniffed Beau's hand, then bounded off again.

Noting the burrs in Moose's smooth brindled coat, he thought, *Cobbler's pegs? Lantana? Blackberries?* He'd better get someone on it or else the neighbours would be on him.

Though the fact that his neighbour was Charlotte Goode had him shifting on his feet.

He might not have been surprised to see one of her parents open the door the day before, but Charlotte? Looking soft and rumpled, chunks of auburn hair falling by her cheeks. All long bare legs in cut-off denim shorts. Loose neck of her old *Muppets* T-shirt showing the delicate triptych of moles along her left collarbone.

The last time he'd seen her was the night before he'd left. She had been in a goth phase; nose ring, lipstick the colour of blackberry wine, long hair cut short making her eyes appear huge. Despite how changed she'd been even then from the girl he'd grown up with, she'd been so… *Charlotte* he'd almost changed his mind.

"Mate?" Matt called.

Beau reached into his back pocket and pulled out his phone, switching off the Bluetooth and holding it to his ear in order to keep himself present. "Sorry. I missed that last bit."

"In dreamland?" Matt asked.

Beau didn't demur.

"That's how we make the big bucks," Matt joked, even while both were well aware that Beau wasn't dreaming in that way these days. "When do you think it'll be done?"

By that, Matt meant, *How long will you be gone?*

"A couple of months," Beau said. "A little less."

"All good, mate. Just, make the most of it. Okay? Your escape to the country."

"It's hardly the country," said Beau, even as he turned and looked out over the valley to the distant beachside towns dotting the coastline.

Matt said, "Anything that's not Sydney might as well be the moon, as far as I'm concerned."

Beau laughed as he knew he was meant to do. "When it's finished, you'll have to bring Tasha and Drew up for a look. You might just change your mind."

"Sounds like a plan. Now, I'd best be off. Five more minutes of work, then it's dad time."

"Give the kids a hug from me."

"Always," said Matt, and Beau heard the note in his voice. The grit, and the tremor.

He could only hope that giving Matt space, and trying to find his way back to what they'd built, he was truly doing the right thing by them both.

"We'll talk later," said Beau.

"Of course, brother." With that, Matt rang off.

Beau slipped his phone into his back pocket and took a slow turn, looking over the land he owned. Acres of greenery, fresh air, sky, dirt. And a view that should make everything else seem inconsequential.

What did he want?

He breathed deep, as if it might come to him. Some thought or seed of understanding he could grab a hold of.

He felt the early evening sunshine, crisp and warm on the back of his neck. Watched Moose bound after a pair of small yellow butterflies. And listened for anything, anyone that might tell him one thing that might make sense of things—

"Beau!"

Beau jerked out of his reverie, as he glanced up to find Charlotte Goode shoving her way through a gap between two rose bushes.

Only in lieu of the bare feet and ragged clothes from the day before, she looked spectacular in a diaphanous top, tight jeans that hugged her long legs, and spiky high heels. A collection of thin gold chains swished elegantly across her collarbone as she moved.

No longer the fierce little kid, or vehement best friend, or gangly teen who'd bloomed overnight into some strange glowing creature who'd made him feel strange and tongue-tied and out of his depth. Yet in the time it took her to pick her way over to him, swearing under her breath, swatting at a bug that flew at her face, he could see echoes of them all.

For a man who had always been so adept at compartmentalising, watching Charlotte pick her way across his yard brought on a wave of nostalgia so wholly disquieting he rocked on his feet.

"Stop," he called, his voice louder than he'd meant.

The adrenaline racing through bloodstream easing as she stopped, her foot mid-step, her arms still swinging. Her gaze met his, questioning.

"You shouldn't be here," he managed, in lieu of, *I can't have you here*, which was what he meant.

So he didn't look like a total head case, he added, "Not in those shoes. It's a worksite."

Charlotte looked down and lifted a stiletto heel as if it hadn't occurred to her that traversing piles of detritus and dug up ground in such a getup might not be ideal.

"Anyway," she drawled, as if the head-case thing was obvious, but no deterrent. "The work trucks were all gone when I got home. Then I saw movement back here, through the sunroom window. Thought, I'd better check to make sure it wasn't a robber."

"A robber."

"I know. Look at me being all neighbourly." She smiled, a flash of white teeth blinding him momentarily. "Did you get your package?"

"My package."

Her head tilted, her gaze narrowing. "The reason you came a knocking on my front door yesterday."

Realising he couldn't keep repeating the ends of her sentences, he gathered himself and said, "Right. Turned out the delivery mob realised it was the wrong place not long after dropping it off. They'd already collected it and taken it back to the warehouse when I came knocking. It will be redelivered tomorrow."

"Wow. Well, great. Crisis averted! Go you."

Hardly. Beau wasn't an engineer in name only. He'd manually stripped more engines and put them back together in new ways than he could remember. Yet, the builders had taken one look at him and sent him on the "important" mission to track the package down. He was prepared to be sent on more "important missions" over the next few weeks, as they endeavoured to keep him out from underfoot.

Which was fine with him. Keeping busy would mean less thinking time. Or, to be more precise, less time spent troubling over the fact that he was struggling to think much at all. For a guy whose entire life had been built on his ability to innovate, that was a precarious space in which to exist.

"So," said Charlotte, "this is the house."

She'd put her hands on her hips, her top lifting to show a sliver of warm tanned skin on her belly. The flash of a sparkle at her navel making him wonder if the goth might have lingered, after all.

Unprepared, *unshielded*, a frisson shot through Beau, a shard of heat and discomfort. Like a last breath of adrenaline. Or something other. Either way, he looked away, joining her in looking up at his build.

She muttered something under her breath along the lines of, "Wow!" before she looked out toward the Pacific. "Remember how this curve of Myrtle Way was nothing but odd ramshackle houses. None of us had aircon, or town water. Just buzzing bees in summer and frosty windows in winter and those wildly beautiful views. The fact that it's becoming

all hoity-toity holiday homes and snazzy gentrification feels highly personal."

She turned back to him, then. And the frisson
was back. He put it down to the shock of seeing
her face—but now her eyes were more knowing,
cheeks sharper, lips fuller. When his gaze moved
back to her eyes, he saw something shift over
her face, as if she was cataloguing the changes
in him, too.

Though the way she breathed—in deep, out
hard—tugged at him in a way he wasn't in any
place to negotiate.

Then she blinked once, breaking the trance,
lifted her chin, and said, "That's a very white hat
you have there."

Taking a moment to catch up, Beau lifted a
hand to his head, where he did indeed sport a
white hard hat. Unlike Charlotte, who when he
wasn't paying attention had begun once again
picking her way across the dug-up lawn, arms
out in balance, high heels wobbling, the chunks
of hair that fell from the loose way she'd tied her
hair swinging by her cheeks.

When she leaped over a pile of rocks in shoes
that had not been engineered with leaping in
mind, Beau's heart, which until this point, had
stayed out of things suddenly lurched painfully.

Arm out, he once again said, "Stop." Then,
"You've entered a construction site. A hard hat
is mandatory. As are flat, enclosed leather shoes,

if not steel-capped boots. If you'd come via the front of the house you'd have seen signs expressing as much."

The front of the house. The way of strangers and acquaintances. Not long-time neighbours, one-time best friends.

"I can go back," she said, pointing over her shoulder. "Come in that way?"

Beau let his hands slowly drop, fully aware how extreme he must seem. Didn't stop the discomfort gripping him any time she moved. "Will you source the requisite safety gear on the way?"

"Nope."

"Then I don't see how that would help."

"Good point." She cocked a hip, one hand thereupon, the other waving at his head. "Aren't they meant to be yellow. The hats?"

"Depends on the worksite. On this one it's blue for carpenters, brown for welders, yellow for general labourers."

"And white is for...?"

"Supervisors. Engineers. Visitors."

"Hmm. So you big wigs can show those blue-collar guys who's boss," she said, taking another step. As if she couldn't help herself.

He was the rule follower, who respected cause and effect, simplicity and clear instructions. While she'd been restless, intensely empathetic, compulsive, and far too stubborn to do as she was told.

When she took another step, and landed on a

stone, her ankle turning, his heart twisted in and over itself as if she'd wavered on the edge of a cliff.

He put it down to the fact that his entire system was up the spout. His usual steady balance in flux.

Until her gaze flew to his, pure crackling energy in those soft moss green eyes, and the frissons he'd felt earlier were mere warm-ups to the electric shock that fizzled down his spine. And he knew that it wasn't all him.

Which was somehow far worse.

"Can you just not?" he growled. "There are hidden dangers everywhere. The lumber is precarious."

Her gaze widened, till they rivalled any Disney princess. "I'm sorry, did you say you have *precarious* lumber?"

He pointed to the stack of old wood before her, rusty nails jutting every which way, and the other pile stacked on the fenceless balcony jutting high above them.

"I see," she said, her mouth twitching. But at least she'd stopped moving.

"So, stay where you are, please. In fact, move back to that nice soft patch of grass. I'd hate to see you get hurt."

And there it was, the underlying truth of what was surely a grand overreaction on his part; the realisation that those under his protection, his care, were in fact in perpetual danger, whether he was on the case or not.

He'd somehow made it through his entire childhood believing he'd been the one to keep total disaster at bay. His vigilance, his unrelenting good grades, his stability—they'd given him a sense of control that had alleviated the state of permanent terror he'd come home to find his parents unconscious, or worse.

When he heard they'd died, while the pain had been sharp, a great burden had lifted. The threads of worry and guilt that had underpinned his ambition had relaxed.

And he'd become complacent.

Then Milly had fallen sick. And he'd not been able to do a thing to help her.

Now here was Charlotte Goode, the wild child next door. Who'd never thought before she acted. Never backed down from a fight. Who'd climb a tree, or cross a stream, or spin with her eyes closed, never once mapping out how it all might go wrong beforehand.

Not that Charlotte was under his purview.

She wasn't even in his life anymore, so much as in his backyard.

And yet…

"I hereby promise not to sue if I stub my toe," she said, hands lifting in surrender. Her voice was teasing, but her gaze was ripe with assurance. Letting him know she'd been messing with him, but was now done.

For while years had passed, and their friendship would never be what it was, once upon a time she had known him. Known what he'd battled. And had had his back.

He nodded his thanks, and his next breath out was a little easier.

"So, Beau," she said, after a few loaded beats.

"Yes, Charlotte."

"It's Charlie now, actually. That's what I go by. These days." She glanced away, as if there was a story there, before she looked back at him, daring him to say different.

For some reason, he felt himself smile a little as he said, "Is it now?" As if the all Charlotte-induced bursts of adrenaline had made him a little giddy.

"It is. Now, yesterday, when you came a knocking on my door, you mentioned you'd taken some time off."

Seemed his adrenal glands weren't yet done. His chest squeezed as he waited for her to ask why. What could he possibly say? *My friend died. After which I became burdened by the weight of existential dread which also left me so untethered it's terrifying.*

Instead she asked, "Time off from what exactly?"

Relieved, he said, "Right. My partner and I run a company called Luculent. We design, test, build and roll out clean alternative power sources. Magnetic, solar, perpetual motion. New technologies as yet unnamed. For travel, industry, city grids. If it requires power and we can help make it clean, we'll try."

"Wow. Did you get that off the brochure?"

"The investment prospectus, actually."

"Ha. That's superhero stuff, Beau. Though Batman wouldn't bother with the hard hat."

"Only because it wouldn't fit over his ears."

She laughed, then. A bark that seemed to surprise even her. Then she tapped a finger against her mouth. And he realised, belatedly, that she was being awfully nice. She was buttering him up. For what, he couldn't even hazard a guess.

"So, this time off, how long might that be?"

A day? Forever? He'd quite like the answer to that one himself.

"The build has another two months. Perhaps a little less. But how about you just tell me what it is you want," he said.

Funny, considering he'd just spent the past half hour staring at a half-finished house he owned but wasn't sure he understood, asking himself the same question.

Then she narrowed her eyes at him and nodded. "First, would you agree that I played rather a big part in setting you up for your amazing superhero career?"

It was Beau's time to laugh, the sound escaping his lips before he felt it coming. "In what way?"

His mind once again went to the last night they'd seen one another.

In all the years they'd known one another it had been the first time he'd ever been in her bedroom. First time in over a year that they'd said more than a couple of words to one another. He was telling her about the scholarship, and that he was leaving the next day.

Charlotte had paced back and forth, shaking her head, arms flying as she said a lot of nothing. Before she'd stopped, looked at him and said, "Go."

"Go?"

"Take it. Take the scholarship. But do not take it for granted. Soak up every moment. Show them who you are. Knock 'em dead. You deserve it, Beau," she'd said, as if she'd known he craved her blessing.

Then she'd pulled him in for one last tight hug, kissed him hard on the cheek, long enough that he'd felt the touch of a tear sliding onto her lips, then given him a shove out her bedroom door and shut it behind him.

"Well," she said, "for one thing, you'd never have been able to afford your first car had I not made those tutoring posters and tacked them up all over town. The same car you drove away in, when you left. Would you say, then, that you owe me?"

"I owe you?"

"Correct. *And* you're taking time off. What

docs that look like for you? Like a day here and there? Or are you on a full-on sabbatical?"

Beau lifted a hand to his neck and squeezed. "Why do I get the feeling you're about to offer me a time-share on the moon?"

Her mouth twisted, her nostrils flaring as she breathed out hard. "Okay," she said, "can I run something—?"

She stopped as her gaze caught on the rustling leaves on the other side of the yard; Moose burst from the bushes and came lolloping up the hill.

After that, everything seemed to happen in slow motion. Charlotte's surprised face. Her hands lifting to protect herself. Moose's massive front paws landing on her chest.

He saw her teeter, pictured her falling backward like a felled tree. Too far for him to catch her, he having told her not to come any closer. His vision shrank to a pinprick, till he heard her laugh.

His vision cleared to find her on her backside, legs akimbo, her face moving side to side to avoid Moose's tongue.

Beau moved in, attempting to heave the dog away and earned a tongue to the nostrils for his efforts.

"Who the heck is this beautiful boy?" said Charlotte, leaning in to rub at Moose's ears and scratching under his collar as he tried to slobber her to death.

Beau managed to stand over Moose, legs locked

around the dog's waist, while Moose looked up at him as if it was his happy place.

"That would be Moose. He belongs to a friend."

Belonged. For he was Milly's. She'd adopted him when she first fell sick, as a distraction for the kids. He'd grown big, fast, and was the single thing Matt had not been able to handle once she'd gone. So Beau had swept in and taken the dog off his hands. The very least he could do.

"I'm looking after him for a while."

"Are you sure that's wise?" she asked, leaning back on her hands and squinting up at him. Moose's whole body wriggled, the swish of his tail connecting hard enough to bruise.

He'd never *had* a dog. Or a cat, or a goldfish for that matter. His parents had been so high most of the time they'd not had the wherewithal to look after him, much less a pet.

He eased off, letting Moose free. The dog, sitting now, looked up at him as if awaiting instruction. As if butter wouldn't melt. Until Beau made a grunting sound that the dog understood as release, and set off, sniffing a path across the patchy back lawn.

"We're still figuring out how to coexist in a way we both find comfortable."

Her eyebrow rose.

He rose one right back.

She blinked, as if in surprise that he'd mirrored her sass.

Then she held out a hand. He reached down and grabbed it, wrist over wrist, fireman style. And heaved her to standing.

She looked strong, all that bristling energy taking up space, but there was nothing to her. As if it was all bluster. Meaning he pulled a little harder than necessary and she let out a whoop before landing.

He held her hand till she settled. It felt small to his big. Unknown. New. It felt like something else, too. Warm, soft, as if it fit just so in his. It felt like relief.

Considering it had been months since he'd felt much in the way of anything at all, his palm began to sweat, his fingertips losing feeling, the whole of him enveloped in a kind of breathless, airless tightness.

Thankfully, with a gentle clearing of her throat, Charlotte peeled her hand from his. She used it to fix her hair, before stepping carefully away, putting distance between them again.

This time when her eyes met his, there was determination therein. "Would you like to have dinner? With me? At my place?"

He opened his mouth. Closed it again.

"That is, if you're staying nearby."

He saw a moment open up between them, then. A chance to pull back, to set up boundaries he'd thought he'd managed to secure the day before.

But she'd stomped over them the moment she pushed through his rose bushes.

But the way she looked at him—a mix of hope, nerves, and bolshie vulnerability—was so very, *very* Charlotte that he found himself saying, "Moose and I are staying in a holiday rental in Maleny till the house is finished, or until Moose eats something crucial and we are forced to leave."

"Nice. So, come over, okay. I'll feed you. My mum was a great cook, do you remember? I'm close. Come and tell me more about your magic engine, and your plans for this place. If you're going to be knocking about here for a couple of months, let's not make this weird."

She was right. It had been weird. Only not for any reasons she might imagine. It was all him. He wasn't sure if his company would be nice. Or if *nice* was what *he* needed right now.

Yet he found himself saying, "What time?"

Her smile was so sudden, so incandescent, it left him feeling as if he'd been hit over the head with a mallet.

"Let's say seven." Then she began backing away, carefully so as not to freak him out, while also giving him no chance to change his mind. Then she was at the rose bushes, and gone.

The sudden lack of her left behind a fresh, sharp kind of quiet, a shallow emptiness that he was certain had not been there before she'd arrived. He pressed into the centre of it, a hard place behind his ribs, then turned to look out over the view once more. Breathing through it as he watched the blue of the softening sky bleeding into the blue of the sea.

Dinner at Charlotte's, he thought to himself, only to find it did not feel weird at all.

As for the rest?

When he breathed deep, there was a moment when he thought he could *almost* catch it. The scent of roses, and greenery, and salty air. And something else. Not a memory, but something close. The one thing that might grab all the disparate parts of himself and bring them back together.

For whatever reason, the fates had decided the only chance he had of finding it was by coming back here.

CHAPTER FOUR

CHARLOTTE WRIGGLED A feather duster at spider webs in the hall, switched on table lamps, fluffed cushions and tossed throw blankets she'd brought out from her bedroom. Marvelling at how little it had taken to make the place feel cosy.

And felt a frisson of guilt at just how long she'd been wallowing. As if living in and amongst her father's things in her father's house was just the right level of punishment for how effectively she'd imploded her own life.

When the truth was she had a roof over her head, was making headway with the back taxes, and her business was steadily growing due to word of mouth from people who believed in her.

She'd not said it out loud for fear a big foot might descend from the clouds, Monty Python–style, and squish her. But she was saying it now: she wanted the Patel/Kent gig.

The guest list would put her business in front of a whole new kind of clientele, and the money would be life-changing.

She could pay off the back taxes in one go, *and* afford to fix the house up a little. Nothing like the monster homes going up around her, but enough to make sure the roof wouldn't collapse, and the dodgy electrics wouldn't burn the place down. In fact, as soon as she'd allowed herself to imagine it, the ideas of how she could zhoosh the place up had been near overwhelming!

She might even have tugged on the loose hallway wallpaper to see how easily it might come off—not very, meaning the hallway was now a disaster. But she could fix that. Then she could safely rent it out, or maybe sell up. She could use the funds to help her relocate to some place that didn't remind her of her father at every damn turn.

And why not Edinburgh, as her mum had suggested? She might even have googled the place a little. It looked beautiful. Wedding-friendly, meaning she could take the bones of her business with her. A nice distance from both here and California. And she could see her mum again.

The *possible* risk of Always the Bridesmaid being tarnished, or even brought down by the spectre of #cakegate was outweighed by the benefits. At least that's what she told herself as she added dressing to the summer salad that would go with the salmon she had in the oven.

Except she was getting ahead of herself. It wasn't in the bag yet.

She'd had no luck finding a man, much less a best one. Then she'd glanced out her side window and seen Beau looking up at his house, all big, and handsome, and solid, and there, and she'd known...

Well, she'd known he was *literally* her only option.

Without him, the rest wasn't going to happen.

Beau Griffin, her ghosts of summer past, was back for a reason. And this, she had decided, was it.

She started as a knock came at the back door. As, for all her renewed enthusiasm, she was nervous as hell.

She and Beau might have been best friends as kids but that was all very much in the past. Despite how charming she'd tried to be, his smiles *still* hadn't quite reached his eyes.

Licking lemon juice from her fingers, Charlie moved out from behind the kitchen bench and through the small dining nook to open the permanently unlocked back door. She wasn't even sure if it could lock.

The thing creaked as she pulled it open to find Beau, two bottles of wine in hand. Which was excellent.

Not so excellent was the fact that while she'd de-glammed, stripping off her girl-boss duds and changing into baggy jeans with a tear in the knee and an oversized Reputation Stadium Tour

T-shirt, Beau had done the opposite. He'd clearly had a shower and washed his hair, evidenced by the finger tracks through his dark hair. He'd also changed into a royal blue long-sleeved T-shirt and clean jeans, both of which clung so lovingly to the shape of him she wasn't sure where to look.

"Hi," she said, her voice offering up a stupid croak.

"Hey," he said back. And even though, behind his glasses, his eyes were wary, the burr in his voice had something climbing her insides like quick-grow ivy.

Till he said, "Only one of your lights is working." He stepped back, gave one of the spotlights a wriggle.

"It's all good! I've got it," she said, turning her back to hide the unhelpful rush of blood to her face as she waved him inside. Yes, the place was falling down around her but it wasn't her fault.

When she rounded the kitchen bench, she saw him duck as he entered, as if by habit. Whereas in the past he'd have stayed hunched over, stooped from the hours he spent on his school laptop, now he stood tall. Comfortable in his skin. As if, having gone away, he'd grown into himself, knew his worth, and owned it.

"Charlotte," he said, his gaze taking in the yellow Formica kitchen, the small sunroom with its cane furniture, the well-scraped wooden floor. "It looks exactly the same."

"You think," she said, not all that keen on thinking on just how *the same* it felt to her much of the time, too. "But since I'm only squatting here for a little while longer, till I get my ducks in a row, there didn't seem any point in going all home decorator on the place."

So there.

"Oh, and it's Charlie."

He glanced at her, his expression serious. Quiet. So *Beau* that her stomach gave a flutter. Only not Beau, for too much time had gone by for her to claim any knowledge of the man at all.

"I think I mentioned earlier that I go by Charlie now."

For *Charlotte* had spent a fortune getting her hair foiled and professionally straightened every six weeks. She'd worn pencil skirts and business shirts. She distracted everyone with all her might to hide her dyslexia so that she might fit into a world she'd imagined would never let someone like her in.

Charlotte had also lost her mind and thrown a handful of cake at her ex-boyfriend—a leech of a human being who used his new bride as a human shield—and missed.

Charlie, on the other hand, dressed how she liked, wore her hair how she liked, and after her game-changing conversation with Julia now told every client right up front that she was dyslexic.

Charlie was a work in progress, which was a good thing.

"Regretting your decision to knock your place down?" Charlie asked, waving a hand at the ancient wood kitchen counter, the cork floors.

"Not for a second."

She mock-gasped, hand to her heart. "Harsh!"

And he smiled. A flash of perfect teeth. He must have had braces at some point, after he'd left. The twisted eyeteeth now in perfect symmetry. Less a cosmetic decision she suspected than a way to wipe away his childhood.

It hit her then, the fact he'd never tried to get in touch her after he'd left—had it been his intention to wipe her from his childhood, too?

"Gimme," she said, shaking off that maudlin thought, and clicking her fingers toward the wine in his hand.

"Suitable?" he asked, turning so she could see the labels, top-notch South Australian Sauvignon Blancs.

"It'll do." She offered up a sassy shoulder shrug. Then, "No Moose tonight?"

"Not tonight. I wasn't sure you'd appreciate him lumbering about, destroying the place."

She looked around at the furniture her mum must have picked out decades before. It might actually have helped.

Then she fixed her T-shirt, after it slid a little off her shoulder, and Beau's nostrils flared. His neck pinked, too. And Charlie once again felt a flicker in her gut. Only this time there was no mistaking what it was. Awareness.

While gratifying—for when wasn't it gratifying to realise someone who gave you tummy flutters felt the same way about you?—she decided to chalk it up to trying to find their new tonal balance. Because awareness, attraction—considering their history, considering *her* history—was not an option.

What she needed him for was far too important to mess up with any of that. And she was not going to screw this up. Not this time.

For once she gave the whispers at the back of her mind air to breathe. They took on the voice of her father, her first roommate, an old boss, and her ex—sheesh, looking at it now, it was if she *gravitated* toward such people—and they told her the myriad ways she'd likely fail. And used it to cool her jets.

She'd feed Beau, get him feeling all warm and full, then she'd hit him with her plan.

"Sit. Dinner is nearly ready." She waved a hand toward the small round dining table she'd set with actual linens and her mother's good china, wanting to set a professional tone. Only now it looked like the perfect set up for an intimate date.

"Can I help?" Beau asked, *not* sitting. Instead he leaned against the kitchen bench, arms braced, hands splayed. The sleeves of his shirt were pushed up to his elbows, revealing strong brown forearms roped with veins. And had he always had such long fingers, such elegant hands?

"Nope," she said, gaze quickly lifting to his face, which was really no better. Because, he had turned out lovely. A crystal cut jaw softened with dark stubble, warm dark eyes, strong straight nose, kissable mouth now slightly open.

When she realised hers was mirroring his, saliva pooling beneath her tongue, she snapped it shut.

"Sit," she ordered. "Please." Thinking of the way he kept telling her to *stop!* in his backyard that afternoon. Had it been about the precarious lumber? Or had he felt a need to keep her at a physical distance then, too?

He smiled at her, while frowning at the same time. As if he was thinking the same. Or maybe he was thinking about something completely different. As for him, those kinds of feelings had *never* been a part of their relationship.

Whereas for her, it kind of had.

She was fifteen when she'd first felt that flutter in her belly where Beau was concerned.

She'd been standing in the high school hallway, getting some books from her locker, when a couple of the "cool" girls had walked past, giggling; one saying she'd just come from the gym, where Beau Griffin of all people had spent the lunch break shooting hoops.

"One after the other," the girl had said on a breathy sigh. "Like his life depended on it. His shirt and shorts were all sweaty, you know, sticking to his chest, his thighs. Whoa, Mumma. Where has he been all our lives?"

Charlie remembered the head rush, the dry mouth, the way her pulse had beat behind her ears, how her fingers hurt from where she'd gripped the door to her locker. Remembered thinking, "Oh, no." Knowing, in some deeply instinctive place that things would never be the same again.

A rap of Beau's knuckles on the table as he curled his long legs beneath snapped her back to the present to find her heart beating a little harder now.

Whereas a regular person would pull out their phone, scroll a little to fill the silence, Beau looked out the window, tested the napkin, breathed the scents from the kitchen. All with such quiet confidence, and stillness. Warmth seeped into her restless bones like a balm.

He'd always been the unruffled to her unquiet. The temper to her temper. Until he hadn't. And the loss of him had felt like a missing limb.

A timer binged and she leaped out of her skin.

Muttering to herself about staying focused, and making good choices, and keeping her head, she grabbed her oven mitts, pulled the old pan from the oven and slid it onto a wooden cutting board.

The oily base had slightly browned, the thyme

appeared crispy, the cream and lemon glaze were glossy and gorgeous. *Perfect*.

She'd take it as an omen. She was a capable, self-governing woman with a dream. Screwing up was *not* her default.

She had this…

"That," said Beau, a half hour later as he put down his knife and fork, "was phenomenal."

Napkin to his mouth, he looked to her. His gaze glinting in the firelight. Because, yes, she'd lit candles. And now the image of that face, all warm eyes and heartache-inducing gorgeousness, was now burned into her retinas for all time.

"What do you think our parents would make of this?" she asked, knowing she might as well have dropped a small bomb between them.

"The two of us having a candlelit dinner?" Beau asked, swiping his finger through the last of the sauce before licking it off his finger.

"It's not *candlelit*," Charlie managed, before leaning forward to blow them out, plunging the room into a dusky intimacy.

Feeling a little overly warm no doubt due to the lingering humidity of the day, she lifted her wine glass to her mouth to find it empty. Oops.

"It's a business dinner," she announced, leaning back farther so as to find some space that didn't have him in it.

"I wasn't aware."

Right. Once conversation had turned to his very not wild university days, to how she'd gone about winning the green card lottery, it had been lovely to fill in the blanks, she'd not quite gotten around to the reason *why* she was liquoring him up. And herself, by the feel of it.

It seemed the time had come!

"I have a proposition for you, Beau. One I am certain you will find most diverting."

"Diverting?" he repeated, a smile in his voice if not his eyes.

She'd have to do something about that. Distracting him away from the dark clouds that followed him was her special skill. And while, by the sounds of it, his life had turned out great, by anyone's measure, it felt crucial that she find a way to do so again.

But first…

"So, Beau Griffin, have you ever been a best man?"

Well, *that* got a reaction. His jaw ticked, and his head jerked back. While for some time he said nothing, the muscles in his neck did rather magical things.

"Or a groomsman," she nudged.

"In a wedding?"

"That's where you'll usually find them."

After another long pause, he said, "Once."

"And how did you find it?"

"I'm not sure I understand the question."

She wriggled on her chair. "Did you enjoy it? Were you any good at it? Were you a follower or a leader? Did you have any particular role? Have you been hankering to have another go?"

He lifted an eyebrow in confusion.

"Okay, let's start with whose wedding was it?"

Again with the long pause. Then, "Matt, my business partner." Then, after a beat, "And my friend, Milly." This time he clenched his jaw tight enough she could hear his teeth creaking.

So, there was a story *there*.

"*Ex*-business partner?" she wondered aloud.

"Current. Why?"

No reason, she thought even as his hand gripped his wineglass hard enough she feared it might break.

What she said was, "The reason I ask is that I have been offered an opportunity. A business opportunity. A pretty significant one. Only it comes with strings that I'm hoping you might be able to…pluck."

The hand gripping the wineglass flexed as if electrocuted. He took a moment to find his words, which turned out to be: "What kind of business might require me to…pluck your strings?"

Hand to heart, Charlie said, "Not *my* strings."

"You want me to pluck *someone else's* strings?"

"*Metaphorical* strings," she elucidated, madly flapping her hands at the universe. Which also helped dissipate the tingles that had shot through her at the thought of all that plucking.

"A bit of background," she said.

Then, in as few—and least likely to accidentally create a double entendre—words as possible, Charlie explained how Always the Bridesmaid had come about, how it worked, her vision as to how it might grow.

She left out #cakegate, because why complicate things?

"That's inventive as hell," he said. "Good for you, Charlie."

The pause before *Charlie* was telling. He'd listened, and respected her request, even while it must have felt strange to him. It made her feel all light and fluffy inside.

She put own her empty wineglass and reached for the glass of water. After draining it she said, "Thank you," while flushing to her damn roots.

Then he said, "I'm just not sure where I come in."

And in the lamplight, her new name on Beau's tongue still bouncing about inside her head, it felt right to offer up some unvarnished truth.

"I had to work, really hard, for any opportunities I had. All the while having to jam my toes in closing doors, climb over impossibly high walls to even get a shot. But this…this is *mine*. I created this while *crashing here* for the past eighteen months. And now someone has stumbled onto what I offer, and given me such a sense of clarity as to what it might one day become."

Beau listened. Even if it made no sense to him, even it was beyond the scope of his own experience, he truly listened. As if he wanted to understand her.

She'd read a meme once, saying something along the lines of "don't talk to me while I'm rubbing my eyes as I won't hear you". That was her ex, Richard, in a nutshell. Even before he'd played his ultimate role of villainous groom.

And she'd *accepted* it. For he'd not yelled at her, never hit her, or called her names. In fact, he'd let her make all the choices; where they lived, what they ate, as if he trusted she'd get it right. Mistaking his laziness for regard, it had taken her far too long to realise how exhausted she was carrying the entire load of their relationship. That he'd "let" her take care of him while he did nothing but flatter her battered self-esteem.

The moment she'd seen it, his brand of manipulation turned on a dime, proving him as ugly as her father had ever been.

Not Beau. His gaze was warm and engaged, his body relaxed, not a fidget to be seen. As if every word she'd ever had to say had its own inherent worth.

Her throat got a little tight. Charlie made for the finish line. "Anushka Patel is that person for me. And, the only way I can take her on as a client is if I also supply a best man."

It only took a second for Beau to join the dots. He shifted, his eyes widening behind his glasses as he leaned back. "You mean *me*?"

Charlie nodded. "And we can negotiate a fair rate for your time."

"Surely you have other men you can ask."

"Other *men*?"

It was a fair question, but just thinking about Richard, about some of the choices she'd made in the past, made her nerves feel all crackly and raw.

"True," she said, "I forgot about the hockey team locked in my basement. Or, if none of them are amenable, there must be an app for this kind of thing?"

Beau said nothing. Loudly. The years between them suddenly feeling as wide as they were deep. But she had one shot at this, so she went for it.

"Here's why you're my number one choice. You ready?"

"Doubtful," he murmured.

"You're available."

Thankfully, he laughed. For a heady second, Charlie thought it might even have reached his eyes, but it was probably the lamplight reflecting off his glasses.

"And you're the right vintage," she added.

"Vintage?"

He lifted a hand to his neck. And she remembered sitting a few rows behind him in assembly, after their falling out, watching the way he massaged his neck, the way his hair fell over his fingers, and feeling as if she might die if he ever stopped.

"Age-wise," she said, sitting up straight, and silently hissing at her inner monologue to take control of itself. "And you'll look the part."

At that, his hand stopped massaging, and his eyes found hers. Direct behind his glasses, no reflections. No glints. So many questions. His voice was a little rough as he asked, "How so?"

Was he really going to make her explain? It seemed he was.

"Well, you're...tall," she said, "which is nice. For a best man. And you're tidy. You don't hunch, or fidget overly much. And clothes don't look terrible when you wear them."

"Clothes don't look terrible?"

She flapped her hands at him, as if it was self-explanatory.

At which point his mouth did that "one corner lift" thing it had done when he'd been standing on her front veranda, looking at her as if she was a happy surprise. The thing that pressed a curve into his cheek. Add the stubble, the slightly too long hair, the way he took up space, all big shoulders and broad chest and...

Hell. Her pulse was racing now. Her lungs struggling to fill. Then her lady parts got in on the action. Heat pooling low, aching. Too many parts of her were reacting now, trying to calm them down was like playing Whac-a-Mole. As if, having seen *no action* since #cakegate, the first chance they had they were preparing to revolt.

"Look," said Charlie, squeezing her eyes shut tight, "I need someone who can follow my instructions, who will understand that I am the boss. Who'll understand that this isn't some party, that it's meaningful for me. Someone I can rely on. Someone I can trust to…"

Her words dried up. Oof, she'd not expected this next bit to be so hard. But in remembering Beau hopping into his bomb of a car and driving off into a future without her, she might as well have stuck her head in a bucket of iced water for the effect it had.

She swallowed, looked him in the eye, and said, "I need someone I can trust to be there when I ask." She let her hands flick out to the sides, then float to her lap. "I know this is a big ask. And despite what we were to one another as kids, we are basically strangers now. But I've found in life that if you don't ask, you don't know. So, this is me. Asking."

Beau said nothing. But she could feel him thinking, at least. Weighing up her request in that thoughtful "look at all sides of the argument, play out every eventuality" way he had about him.

Thankfully, being Beau, it took about five seconds, before he said, "What would it entail, exactly?"

"I don't have that worked out as yet, but I imagine meeting the groom and the other groomsmen socially as to establish rapport. A suit try-on or two. Rehearsal dinner, bucks' night, but perhaps not. Depends on what they need from us. Then the big day. It's less than six weeks away, meaning it would all be done and dusted before you're done here."

That was all she had.

Now everything she wanted depended on what he said next.

He said, "Sure. Of course. Why not?"

She pressed her chair back with a scrape and stood, more energy coursing through her than she'd felt in months. "Are you serious? You will actually be a pretend best man at the wedding of a person you do not know for me?"

Shut up, Charlie! Just say thank you, then maybe have him swear a blood pact.

By then Beau had pushed his chair back and also stood. He tossed his napkin to the table and said, "It seems so."

Charlie felt as if a pair of hands grabbed her by the waist, lifted her from her chair and propelled her around the table then, for suddenly she was leaning over Beau, flinging her arms around his neck and hugging the life out of him.

They'd had *no* personal space as kids. Always

bumping shoulders or linking arms as they traipsed over hill and dale of their backyards. Feet tangled as they lay in her backyard, star gazing, hands colliding as they dipped into a shared box of popcorn while snuggled beside one another in the break in the fence at the local drive-in. She'd sat on his lap as he'd taught her how to drive, long before either had a license, for Pete's sake!

But this? Charlie came to from her burst of adrenaline to find her head buried in Beau's neck, drinking in a heady mix of fresh cotton, and warm male skin, and something light and citrusy. His hair tickled her temple. His stubble scraped her cheek.

Only then did she notice his arms strong and warm around her back.

It had been so long since she'd held someone. Or been held. With abandon and trust. Not measuring how long it should be before she let go. Which was why Charlie stayed there a beat too long. Several in fact.

Her body a comma curled into his. The heat of him burning through her clothes, till his heart beat in syncopation with her own.

Her inner monologue cleared its throat, waking her from the heady fog. And she pulled away, pushed more like. Once clear, she tugged at her T-shirt and attempted a smile.

"Thank you," she managed. "I mean it, Beau. This will be life-changing."

In a good way for once, she hoped with all her might.

"Happy to help," said Beau, running a hand through his own hair till it was more than a little mussed. Then rolling out a shoulder, as if trying to shake off the same warmth that was still moving through her, too.

When Charlie found herself looking at him, for no reason other than she liked doing so, she shook her head and said, "Look, I've kept you far too long. How about I box you up some leftovers. For tomorrow night. Or for Moose."

"That'd be nice."

Charlie hotfooted it into the kitchen, her skin still tingling like crazy, her blood going more than a little haywire. Because he'd said yes. Because she might actually pull this off. And because being in Beau's arms had felt like heaven.

Her hands shook as she fussed about finding the right-sized Tupperware. Only to spin from the cupboard to find him at her sink, their dirty dishes piled up on the bench as he rolled up his sleeves a little higher before slinging a tea towel over his shoulder and turning on the hot water.

"What are you doing?"

"You cooked. I clean. That's how it works, right?"

Not in her experience. But since her parents had never put in a dishwasher, she wasn't about to say no.

Once she was done wrapping, she snuck the tea towel from Beau's shoulder, catching his eye as she snuck around him, the dark glint, the slight lift at the corner of his mouth, before she took over drying.

"Anything else I can do?" he asked. No doubt noting the wonky cupboard door over the stove, the water stain on the ceiling.

Grateful for the help washing, but very sure she could look after herself otherwise, she all but manhandled him out the back door. Everywhere she touched him, his arm, his back, she could feel the shape of him, the give of hard muscle, the warmth seeping through his clothes, imprinting itself on her palms.

On the back landing, he glanced up at her broken light.

"Ignore it," she commanded.

He looked back, his face danger close, as he shot her a quick smile. "It would take me two minutes."

"And yet, it's not your problem. It's mine. I like it that way."

His smile dropped away. Later, when she was alone, trying to shut the back door so that it didn't fly right open, she might kick herself. But right now, she needed to finish this evening with Beau agreeing to help her with the Patel/Kent gig, and that was all.

At the bottom of her rickety back steps, the

very ones they used to hide under as kids, he looked back.

"Thank you for dinner."

"And thank you for agreeing to help me out. You have no idea how grateful I am."

"I have some idea," he said, before he strode toward the rose bushes.

And if by that he meant the effusiveness of her hug, well damn.

"Beau!" she called when he was halfway across her backyard. "You don't live there anymore, remember. Build site. No hard hat. Many dangers."

He lifted a hand, then spun forty-five degrees and headed up the side of her house. And was gone.

Charlie watched the space, even though she couldn't see him. Feeling as if he'd grabbed a hold of a loose thread in her jumper, unravelling it, and her, as he went.

Charlie squeezed her eyes shut for a moment, before she spun back inside the house. She went straight for her phone, grabbed it and texted Anushka. So freaking exhilarated was she, she didn't even check for typos.

The perfect best man all lined up. We're in!

Seconds later a spate of emojis exploded into her messages.

It was done. The ball rolling. No going back.

A mix of relief, and mild terror fought it out inside her, as Charlie realised one way or the other, the safe, *slowly slowly* pattern she'd fallen into was all about to change.

CHAPTER FIVE

BEAU COULDN'T RIGHTLY say what had convinced him to agree to Charlotte's harebrained scheme. For he wasn't in any place to be a person's so-so man much less one's best.

A mix of things, most likely. A need to fill his empty days with more than "fake missions" from the builders. A throwback to the way he'd always ended up bundled along on her "adventures." Surprise that she was living in her father's house.

Charlotte had always been a force of nature; she changed a room simply by walking into it. But as far as he could see, she'd done nothing to update the place since moving in. It was a time capsule, and not in a good way. For while she and her mother had always been tight, Charlie and her father could not have been more at odds.

The man had called Charlotte names, constantly. Picked on her for being a minute late, for laughing too loudly, for scraping a knee. And he constantly brought up Beau's grades, then asked for Charlotte's results, knowing they'd not measure up in his eyes.

As a kid he'd thought of Professor Goode as being a bit of a storybook ogre, but looking back the man was a pitiful bastard who'd systematically tried to tear his daughter down. Likely because no matter how hard he tried, to the outside eye he never made a dent on her.

But Beau knew that wasn't true. For it was his shoulder she'd cried on.

He remembered the day she'd told him about her dyslexia diagnosis—how excited she was to have a reason to give her father for being "dumb." Only it had made her father even more enraged, for how dare a child of his not be naturally brilliant? After that she'd given up on even thinking about going to university.

Till then it had been their joint plan; for him to take a gap year and work, so that they could head to uni together. A plan he'd been the one to break.

When she'd asked for his help, could he say anything but, "Of course"?

Then she started sending him voice messages at unearthly hours of the night, links to draft schedules colour-coded in bright pastels with sparkly graphics, created by someone called Julia, and text messages he imagined her reading three times before sending, the way she had as a kid.

Charlotte: Schedule okay with you so far?

Beau: Yes.

Charlotte: If there are any conflicts, the sooner I know the better.

Beau: It's fine.

Charlotte: Your enthusiasm is infectious.

And:

Charlotte: Adding a suit fitting for four o'clock next Tuesday.

Beau: I am in possession of suits.

Charlotte: And yet. Groomsmen match.

Beau: Then how will people know that I am the "best" one?

Charlotte: Prove it.

He got on board with:

Beau: My electrician tells me you traipsed through the rose bushes this afternoon.

Charlotte: Dobber!

Beau: He said you weren't wearing a hard hat. Or covered shoes.

After that came a voice message: *Did he not tell you that I found a recipe for banana muffins that is both dog and human friendly? And since bananas contain both magnesium and potassium and...some other thing that is brain-calming, I thought it might be good for Moose. And by way of Moose, Moose's babysitter. But you weren't there so I gave them to your builders, and if you're going to be all "wear a hard hat next time" about it, then that's the last banana muffin you'll ever see from me.*

Lastly, a final text:

Buckle up, buttercup, tonight is the bride and groom meet & greet. A club in Noosa. Dress pretty. My place at six. I'll drive.

He wondered if he could slink back to Sydney, tell Matt he was all better, and forget the whole thing.

That night, after checking on the build, Beau knocked on Charlotte's back door, only for the thing to bounce on its hinges and open right up.

"Charlotte?" he called.

No answer. A frisson of something dark and slippery slithered through him.

Louder, he tried, "Charlie?"

"Come in!" she called. "I'll be a minute!"

A deluge of relief followed. Enough that he wondered if it was too late to pull out.

For telling her to stop walking through a construction site filled with hazards because he was terrified that everyone he cared for might die on his watch was on him. Fretting over her busted back door and broken back light was surely a step too far.

Then he made his way into the kitchen, noting the curling edges of a seven-year-old calendar on the wall, the frosted glass cabinet filled with her father's coffee mugs. And he knew he was exactly where he ought to be.

Which, considering the past few months, was not a small thing.

Charlotte's head popped out of a room in the hallway so Beau wandered that way. She held up a finger, motioned to the phone at her ear, as she said, "Isla, listen to me. Your bridesmaid dresses are not *puce*, they are dusky rose. And they are gorgeous. The next time your mother-in-law tries to undermine your choices, imagine me kicking her in the ankle just before the mother son dance."

Her eyes caught his, and he gave her a thumbs-up.

Her mouth stretched into a quick dazzling smile.

Then her gaze dropped as she gave him a quick once-over. Her gaze paused on his chest, his thighs, his neck. When it met his one more, the bob of her throat and the way she tucked her hair behind her ears made it clear he was up to scratch.

Lucky, because he'd actually put effort into getting ready that evening; shaving, shining his shoes, had the rest of his clothes couriered from his apartment in Sydney. He wanted to represent her ably. And if it meant he got to experience that look in those eyes, well that wouldn't be entirely terrible, either.

A minute later Charlotte rushed down the hall.

"Okay, let's do this!" She began riffing names of those they were to meet that night—bridesmaids and groomsmen, their relative family situations, jobs, relation to the bride and groom.

Not that he heard a word for his brain was filled with the sight of her in her knee-high black boots, short black dress over white button-down, her hair in a crown of braids wrapped about her head with curls springing free at her temple and neck.

She gave wholesome milkmaid meets Wednesday Addams, and for a man who'd never thought he'd had a particular type, he knew in that second he'd been wrong.

He cleared his throat. Looked anywhere but at her. Reminded himself this was Charlotte. *Charlie*. A very old friend. For whom he was doing a favor she deemed important.

They'd never been the other thing.

Yes, he'd had "crush type" feelings at one time, but he'd very much kept them under wraps. Choosing to focus even harder on his studies and take up basketball after reading a research article that suggested exercise was a healthy way to redirect such things.

"What?" she said, and Beau realised she'd stopped halfway up the hall, her hand in her bag, her expression wary. No doubt because he was staring at her like he'd been hit over the head with a mallet.

"All okay with Isla?" he asked, spinning a finger in the air before herding her back up the hall so they could head out the front door to the car.

"Sure. Maybe. Her mother-in-law is a dragon. My role there with that client is to make the mother-in-law hate me so she leaves Isla alone."

"Is that normal?"

She shot him a grin over her shoulder, and he felt it in his gut. "Always the Bridesmaid is hardly normal. We're not wedding planners, we look after the jobs no one else wants, or the ones they didn't know they needed. We traverse the emotional landmines. Mitigate the 'in the moment' dramas. Have the hard conversations with members of the outer circle so that the bride and groom can enjoy their big day."

"Sounds consuming."

"It's much easier when you don't have skin in the game. I'll drive!" she said as she let him out the front door.

He watched to make sure she locked up. "I'm happy to drive. My car's out front."

"And I'm the boss of this show. I want everything to be as easy for you as it can possibly be so that you do not regret agreeing to help for a single second."

Too late, he thought, then watched as she noticed the car parked next to her dented Cooper S.

"Are you kidding me?" she asked, her eyes wide, voice giddy as she walked toward his car as if she was being beamed. Her fingers air-traced the sleekly curved bonnet. "What is this thing?"

"This is Lucky. A prototype. Concept car. One of a kind. Cars like this are usually no more than a chassis on a rotating platform at a car show, but Lucky is the next step. She currently runs on our patented electric engine; but she's been built to swap straight to the Luculent Engine we have in the testing pipeline right now."

Lucky and the Luculent Engine were his passion projects. The creations he'd nurtured from seed to fruition since he'd first envisioned the tech a decade ago. The engine was the last thing he'd seen to completion before Milly passed, before his muse tossed its hands in the air and said, *Everything ends anyway, so why bother?* The thinking so redolent of his parents, it bothered him.

"Do you let *Moose* hop in this thing?"

Beau nodded.

"Wow. That's…brave. Can I drive?" Charlotte asked.

Beau tossed his keys skyward, watched as her eyes lit up, before he caught them again. "Not on your sweet life."

He went around to the passenger door, gently moved her out of the way, and pressed a button on the key so that the passenger door swooped open like a wing. She jumped back, into him, an impressed oath falling from her lips.

Even in her high-heeled boots, the top of her head just reached his nose, meaning he had no choice but to drink her in—the scent of hair, some botanical aroma, and that warm sweet something that was purely her.

He ushered her inside the car.

Once she was settled, he jogged to the driver's side door and slid inside.

Lucky's design was Matt's field, but he'd kindly built it so Beau didn't have to twist himself up like a pretzel in order to fit. The interior details were clean and elegant, vintage throwbacks mixed with proprietary clean tech that made other designers salivate with envy. The colour—a dark bronze—was Milly's favourite. Making Lucky, to their minds, the perfect Luculent vehicle.

Beau turned her on, ran both hands over the wheel, before easing the car down the curving driveway, avoiding the overhanging greenery along the way.

"Oh, wow." Charlotte laughed beside him. "I'd forgotten that you did that."

"Did what?"

She lifted her hands and copied the way he'd traced the steering wheel. "Remember? You'd do that with your first car, giving thanks she started at all."

He ran his hands over the wheel again as they reached the front gate, lifting the memory from the recesses of his mind. The cracked leather under his hands, the flicker of bitumen through the small hole in the floor. The car in worse shape than he'd hoped, his mother having found the first few hundred dollars he'd saved and using it to buy dope, meaning he'd had to choose a car held together with duct tape.

Should he be doing this? Could he?

He flicked a glance toward Charlotte, to see her snuggling into the sports seat, eyes closed, beatific smile on her face.

He could do this. In fact...

After checking both ways were clear, he shot out onto Myrtle Way so fast Charlotte whooped.

A little under an hour later, they'd parked the car on a side street in Noosa.

"Will Lucky be safe here?" Charlie asked, eyes worried, clearly having become rather fond of the car.

"She'll be fine." Beau pressed his thumbprint

to the key, locking the doors and setting the security features.

Their publicity team had also made a good case for organic interest, so having the Luculent badge on display was the least he could do for his company while doing nothing at all.

Charlie waited on the footpath, smiling as he joined her, then they began walking in tandem down the road, taking in the distant sound of gentle waves and the briny scent on the air.

When Charlotte's hand slipped into the crook of his arm, Beau started.

Taking it for distress, she quickly removed her hand and stepped away. When the truth was her touch had sent an electric shock right through him, and rogue sparks still skittered through his system.

"Sorry," she said, shooting him a quick glance. Then, "It's a dyslexia thing."

He lifted an eyebrow in question.

"When I was living in the States, I found this amazing dyslexia therapist. She believed it affects my spatial awareness, and how I read body language. It explains the way I used to manhandle you."

"I think I'd remember being manhandled—"

"It was constant!" she said, giving a little skip down the footpath. "I was always sliding my hand through your elbow. Hugging you. Curling my feet around yours. I could barely leave you alone."

He remembered. His parents had moved into that house, an inheritance from a grandparent he'd never met, when he was seven. The first time he'd seen Charlotte she'd been up a tree. After a few minutes spent casing him as he sat below, she'd leaped down, grabbed him by the arm, held a finger to her lips, then dragged him into the brambles down the hill to show him a veritable field of small yellow butterflies that must have just shed their cocoons.

At first it had been a shock, all that energy, and friction inside his space. But soon he'd come to expect her easy affection. Then to crave it. For he got none of that kind of thing at home.

Before he could stop himself, Beau held out the crook of his elbow. "Come on, then."

With a surprised smile, Charlotte stepped back in, sliding her hand into the nook.

"Now, test time," she said, as they slowed their pace down the footpath. "Who are we meeting?"

"We're *meeting* people?"

Laughing, Charlotte rocked closer, giving him a shove with her hip. "Come on. I've sent you enough voice messages about tonight. You must have been dreaming their names."

He could hear her voice in his head: Anushka and Bobby. Anushka's bridesmaids, her cousins Phyllida and Jazmin. Bobby's groomsmen, work mates Jeff and Lenny. But he looked to the sky as if he might find them there.

"Stop playing," she said. "You're making me nervous."

And he could feel it in her, that infectious Charlotte energy. The restlessness of her steps, the way her fingers wrapped tighter around his arm.

"Okay. No more games," he promised.

She shot him a quick look, as if she thought he might have meant something else by it, before she looked straight ahead and said, "It's not far."

What had she been thinking he meant? He'd been imagining the Uno pack she kept in a metal box under her back steps, so worn down they knew the cards by the creases and tears. Or had she been thinking of the one time they'd played something entirely different.

The summer before his senior year, not long after he'd taken up basketball in order to sweat off the way he'd begun to feel about her, she'd found them some new friends. Kids she worked with at the vintage vinyl record store.

He didn't have much in common with them, as none were interested in what they might do after school bar get their license and swap fake IDs for real ones. But he liked that they liked Charlotte. How they looked to her, saw her spark. How relaxed and happy she seemed.

One afternoon they'd met up at the local playground with chips, picnic blanket, and Frisbees. Their laughter that had gone on into the evening after one of the guys brought out a bottle of gin that had them all coughing and falling over one another well into the evening.

Beau hadn't touched the stuff, not after seeing how his parents would drink till they passed out. But Charlie had, swigging and laughing with the rest of them.

Once the bottle was empty, someone suggested a game of spin the bottle.

He remembered, with such clarity, looking up, his gaze inexorably finding Charlotte sitting directly across the blanket. Her eyes were on him, wide and diamond bright.

His chest had boomed so hard under the power of that look he'd thought it might burst. Only he had no idea what she was thinking, or feeling. Only that their gazes had caught. Tangled. Linked at some multidimensional level. The moonlight obfuscating so much, but not everything. Not the way his heart had thundered in his chest, or the rise and fall of her chin as if her breaths had not come easily enough.

Only she'd been drinking. So how could he, or she, be sure?

So while he'd have given just about anything to have his bottle land on her, to be able to lean over that blanket and press his lips to hers, even once, when the bottle had spun, he'd reached out, grabbed the bottle, walked it to the nearest council bin, and let it drop.

As if the lot of them had been feeling the tension, and were glad to be rid of it, they'd fallen about, laughing in relief. And they'd moved on to something else.

While he knew that letting fate decide whatever happened between them that night would have been all kinds of wrong, afterward he and Charlotte were never quite the same.

His final year of school, his studies had consumed him. They had to, if he had any chance of earning a scholarship to pay for the engineering degree he had his heart set on. While she'd begun spending every afternoon working or hanging out at the record store. Until one day, when he passed her in the hall at school, she'd not even noticed him.

"This is it," she said now, when they reached a dark brick building with fluorescent flamingos and palm trees twice Beau's size decorating the facade. Stepping back to catch his eye, her hand still gently resting in the crook of his elbow, she said, "You ready?"

"Anushka and Bobby," he said. "Anushka's bridesmaids are her cousins Phyllida and Jazmin. Bobby's groomsmen are Jeff and Lenny."

Her resultant smile was worth every moment of discomfort that led up to it.

Hours later Charlie leaned her forehead against the mirror in the passenger seat of Beau's space car. The cocoon of the ergonomic seating and the quiet hum of the electric engine acted like some kind of relaxation app, all but rocking her to sleep.

It might also have been that after the buildup to the night, she was exhausted due to her lingering concerns regarding risk versus reward associated with Anushka's offer, as well as wondering whether Beau would find anything in common with a bunch of reality TV stars and F1 motorheads.

She needn't have worried.

After the round of introductions, during which Charlie made it clear that she was the boss, and Beau was a very brilliant, very wonderful, very much appreciated old friend doing her a favour, Anushka had asked what Beau usually did with his time. When he'd explained he was cofounder of a company called Luculent, Bobby the F1 driver and his "car mad" friends had lost their minds.

Beau had done her proud, listening more than he spoke, which was pure Beau, and when it was his turn to speak, he'd been erudite, funny, and warm.

And anytime she caught his eye, checking in to see if he needed rescuing, he'd given her a look as if making sure *she* was okay.

If that had made her heart go all a flutter, it was only because she was usually the one doing the checking. It was the crux of her job, after all. Her relationships, too, if she was honest with herself. Richard had seen her coming from a mile off.

"Penny for your thoughts?"

Charlie blinked, then shifted to face Beau, to find his long fingers resting lightly on the wheel, at ten and two. Such the rule follower. It made her smile.

He shot her a quick glance, his brow furrowing in question, before his gaze moved back to focus on the dark winding road.

Remembering he'd asked her a question, Charlie said, "Nothing much. Stream of consciousness, mostly." Then, "Starting with what a revelation *you* were tonight."

He laughed, the sound deep and husky. "Am I detecting a hint of surprise?"

"Uh, yes! You weren't exactly a chatty Cathy when we were kids. Too much going on up here." She pointed to her forehead.

"While you never stopped talking," he said.

"I had a lot to say. Lucky for me, you were such a good listener. Still waters ran deep."

They still do, she thought. She watched as the moonlight flickering through the trees overhead washed over his face, kissing his strong features, playing over his glasses like a movie. Then said, "My panic decision to ask you to help was truly inspired."

A smile hooked at the corner of his mouth, and

it did such nice things to his already nice face that she shifted on her seat.

"Anyway, in case I forget to say so later," she said, stifling a yawn. "Thank you, for exceeding my expectations."

"Stop," he said, "before my ego spins out of control."

"Okay," she said, then went back to looking out the front window.

After a few moments, Beau said, "I can't imagine what it must be like having to navigate all of that on your own."

"That was nothing. That was friends at a party—stress level minimum. The wedding day—that is war games in fancy dress. It's the Wild West."

"You love it, though," he said, and it wasn't a question.

"I really do. Even the truly unexpected moments, where I am the only one between complete disaster and hilarious wedding memory, are mostly fun." When her thoughts went to #cakegate, she was actually surprised. For it actually had been a couple days since she'd even thought about it.

"What about you?" she asked. "What do you love most about your job? Apart from driving around in a sexy rocket car?"

He laughed then, a soft chortle that felt surprisingly intimate. Then took quite a lot of time to say, "There's a lot to like, actually."

"Such as?"

"It's ours, for one. Meaning we've been able curate the shape of it. The scope. The size. And our roles within. I get to be hands-on, to spend time on-site playing with materials, and seeing how our designs come together. Our name is an invitation that gets me in front of great minds. Our setup means I can hole up in my studio, sketching out ideas day and night."

"Wow. That's my dream to be that autonomous. To have that level of respect in my work."

She'd thought she'd been on her way in her last job, but with time and distance, and after how readily they'd cut her free, she had to admit she'd been dreaming. Stuck in a rat race, dancing to other people's tunes. Which just wasn't…her.

"If I had all that," she said, "I'm not sure I'd ever want to take time off."

A full minute went by, during which Charlie somehow found herself imagining Beau wiping a grease-stained hand across his sweaty brow, those long fingers working at something deep inside an engine, before he said:

"The best part? Building it alongside close friends. Matt, my business partner, he and I did our degrees together at university. Milly, too."

Matt and Milly. "As in Matt and Milly for whom you were best man?"

His hands shifted on the wheel, gripping a little harder as he said, "The very same."

"Aw. That's so nice. And what was that like, their wedding? Big? Intimate? Destination? Did you do anything terrible to Matt at the bucks' party? Was Milly a total bridezilla? I met enough of those working events in San Fran. Funny, since starting Always the Bridesmaid, all my brides have been lovely."

Another reason why working for herself was such a kick. She could choose what behaviour to accept. And never get herself in a situation where she worked for someone who wished her ill. Which seemed like the baseline, really.

When she realised Beau had not answered her pepper of questions, she looked over at him to find his hand was squeezing his neck, hard. "Beau?"

"Can we not?"

Charlie blinked. "Not...?"

"Talk about the wedding."

"Oh, sure." Charlie nibbled at her lip, keeping mum for a good fifteen seconds, before saying, "Unless there's something about it. I ought to know what would affect your ability to do the job—"

"Milly died."

Charlie flinched, a small shocked sound shooting from her lips. For a while she'd picked up that there was something amiss. But she'd *not* seen that coming. "Oh, Beau. I'm so sorry. Back then?"

Please no. If she'd asked him to be best man after that...

"A few months ago," he managed.

Which was not better. "May I ask how?"

Was asking even the right thing? Trapped in the cocoon of the car, the soft sounds and gentle sway and darkness outside lit only by the headlights made it feel okay. As if they were the only two people in the world.

"Cancer. Fast. She and Matt... They were just right for each other. Both blisteringly smart, and open, and for whatever reason they took me on, too. Business partner. Best man at their wedding. Godfather to their two kids. And—"

He stopped. Breathed out hard.

"Hey," she said, reaching out to rest a hand on his shoulder, before pulling back. Hearing her therapist's kind voice—*Body language, personal space*. "It's okay. We don't have to talk about it."

His eyebrows rose. "I think that horse has already bolted."

"Yeah, it kind of has." Then, "Is *that* why you're here? Why you're taking time off?"

"The simple answer is yes."

"You're grieving," she said, and that something amiss, the way his smiles never reached his eyes, when in the past that had been one of her favourite things about him, now made such sense.

He said nothing. But he didn't need to.

She'd looked up the five stages of grief, after her father had died, trying to work out what she *ought* to be feeling. The anger bit she got. Anger with him, with her mum for sweeping them off to the United Kingdom, where her family were from. With herself for not letting his words wash off her back like the formless venom they were.

If she were guessing, she'd say Beau was somewhere in bargaining/depression spectrum. For surely tearing down his parents' house was connected. Had he truly grieved their loss? Her mother hadn't seen him at the small funeral, or heard anything from him when the house had sold.

Not that she was any expert when it came to facing up to the wounds of one's childhood. Hell, her father's office remained untouched by her, or by her mother. Anyone wandering past it might think it a shrine, rather than an example of how excellent they both were at pretending out of sight meant out of mind.

Beau slowed and turned his car into her driveway, then let the engine hum to a stop. And the interior lights slowly turned on till a golden light shone over them, making the space seem smaller.

She wanted to say thank you, again, *and* that she hoped he'd feel better soon, but both seemed such inconsequential ways to sum up what she wanted to tell him.

So instead, she leaned over to kiss him quickly on the cheek.

Only he must have seen her move, as he turned at the last, and her lips brushed the corner of his mouth. The rough scrape of stubble and the soft give of his lips sent shards of embarrassment and liquid heat rushing through her. And yet she stayed, the both of them rigid with surprise.

When the embarrassment bit outweighed the other, she pulled back, said, "Well, good night!" then started jabbing at the door, trying to find her way out.

Beau's door opened and he slid easily from his seat.

Charlie's leg jiggled madly as she waited, and when her door winged open she shot outside in a gaggle of legs and bag and hair in her eyes.

Beau stood by the car, hands in the pockets of his suit pants, looking tall and solid, cool as a cucumber. He also had a small smile at the corner of his mouth, as if her flutters were amusing.

"So," she said, not daring to see if the smile reached his eyes. Instead, she looked at the sky, the trees rustling in the night breeze. "Thanks again for tonight. You were amazing. And this is going to be such fun! And I so appreciate your help…yep." She clicked her fingers at him and finished with, "I'll be in touch with next steps."

Beau lifted a hand to his heart. "I'll feel every buzz."

Charlie stared at him, feeling the buzz herself. All over. Flickers, sparks, making it hard to stand still.

Then she realised he meant his phone. In his

pocket. When it buzzed. With her incessant messages.

"Great, great, great!" she said, sounding like a hyperactive hen. Then, "And thank you, for telling me about Milly."

Shut up! her internal monologue insisted.

I can't!

"Please let me know if I push too hard, or ask too much. I can be like that; a little over gungho when I get excited about things. I mean, you know me."

"I do," he said, as if he did. Still. Not merely that he *had*, a really long time ago. When they were both unformed, both so young. But that he saw her now, as she was.

"Okay," she squawked. "Well, good night."

She could have stepped back, waved, slipped inside the house. But she felt as if she were floating outside of her own skin, watching herself from above as she stepped in, lifted a hand to Beau's chest, tipped up on her tiptoes and kissed him on the cheek again.

This time she hit her mark.

The brush of his soft stubble against her cheek brought her back into her body with a slam. Till she could feel everything. The flutter of her lashes against her cheeks, like butterfly wings. The scent of his skin in her nostrils. The feel of him under her hand, which had landed on his chest.

When she pulled back, their eyes met. No smile

there still, but there was no room between the sparks of heat, and silvery moonlight, and history that seemed to swirl therein.

"Good night, Beau."

"Good night, Charlie."

Then with one last long look, he shook his head, and jogged around the front of his car.

She lifted her hand in a wave, then somehow made it to the door on legs that didn't feel quite right. He waited until she was inside before he drove away.

As she washed off her makeup, got into her pj's, and brushed her teeth, her mind went over the night again and again.

Her arm in his as they'd walked to the club. The way he'd kept her hand when they'd gone inside, so that he could shield her from the swarm of bodies. How charming and on song he'd been with her clients, making her look so good.

And now she understood that glint of grey he carried with him, now she knew that he was grieving, deeply, for a friend. Was it wrong that it only made him more appealing?

Not that it mattered. For outside of his work on behalf of Always the Bridesmaid, Beau Griffin's "appeal" was irrelevant. Soon his house would be finished and he'd head back to his real life— one of luxury cars, and big business, and "close friends" she'd never know.

Or would he? He'd not said what his plans for

the house were when he was done. Was he planning on renting it out? Keeping it as a holiday home? Was he even planning on going back to Sydney? What if he stayed? Then they'd be proper neighbours all over again.

No. No, no, *no*!

His plans mattered not a jot. For *she* was leaving. On her own terms, and good ones, this time. Not kicked out of home by an unsatisfied man who'd used her as a mental punching bag, not "vowing never to return," or being chased out of town, out of a life she'd thought she finally had a handle on, because she'd made such a colossal error of judgement.

Leaving, starting somewhere fresh, some place with no intrinsic baggage, would be the opposite of screwing up, or self-sabotage, or reacting to her situation. Making it the very best thing she could do for herself.

It was after midnight when she finally fell face down on her bed, then climbed under her bedsheets. And while her mind raced in circles, most of them around Beau Griffin, by the time she did fall asleep, she slept like a rock.

CHAPTER SIX

BEAU DIDN'T MAKE any unnecessary trips to the house over the next couple of days. Though what constituted *necessary*, he couldn't honestly say.

Instead he stayed near the rental. Did a little sudoku, scrolled funny cat videos. He took Moose for a walk, then another, doing as had been suggested and putting a little less pressure on himself where the dog was concerned. Trying the same for himself, he passed up his usual hot black double shot espresso and tried a decaf almond "milk" latte in a holistic café in Montville, and quickly decided it wasn't for him.

All of which was done in the effort at not thinking quite so much about Charlie.

Charlie. When had he started thinking of her as such? Hearing Anushka rave about her. Or when he'd gone into town, found the record store she used to work at, and the guy behind the counter had recognised him, saying, "Hey, aren't you Charlie's Beau?"

Or was it when she stepped up, leaned in, and kissed his cheek.

For all the times they had been all over one another as kids—wrestling, arm in arm, snuggling under her back stairs on cold winter nights—*Charlotte* had never done that.

Now he couldn't stop replaying it, over and over again in a hypnotic loop. The way her eyes had gone wide and soft all at once. The way her fingers had curled gently against his chest. The way she'd breathed deeply, as if gathering the scent of him. The feel of her lips, soft and pliant, lingering. The small sound she'd made, as if kissing him had given her relief.

Then, when he dragged himself out of the loop, he'd think of Milly. Or, to be precise, he'd think of Matt at home missing his wife. Somehow getting through each day, taking care of their kids, with help from Milly's devastated mum, all of their hearts in shredded ribbons.

While he was going to nightclubs, laughing, making friends with race car drivers, swaying to music he'd never heard, Milly never would again.

One thing had nothing to do with the other. He knew that. Didn't stop the grit that gathered inside him with every turn of the story. When it became too much, in need of a distraction, he opened his work email for the first time since going north.

Only to find it was lighter than he might have

expected. As if it was being deliberately curated by a concerned business partner, who had more than enough on his plate than to be adding that.

He'd opened an email to tell said business partner such, when Moose jumped up, a great paw landing on the laptop and sending an email that went something like "ncjosabuisari albiuwer".

Beau ruffled the dog's ears, before gently pushing him back to the floor. Where he panted happily, before rolling on his back for a tummy rub.

A minute later Beau's phone rang.

"You emailed!" Matt announced, as if trumpets and revelry would be an appropriate accompaniment.

"Moose emailed," Beau explained, giving Matt a moment to actually read the thing.

"Worrying," said Matt, "if that had been you. And yet, it was from your email address. Meaning unless the dog has learned your password, you had checked in."

Beau sat back in the too small chair at the too small desk in the corner of the too small nook in his summer rental, and remembered how nice it felt to be in one's own office. Honestly missing the converted warehouse in which Luculent resided for the first time since he'd left.

Not the setup, or the white noise of staff busy at work, but those early days when they'd first moved in and he'd been able to make the space exactly what he needed it to be in order to *think*.

To imagine, to create, without the weight of time, or money, or guilt, or worry hanging over him.

He pictured one of the huge bedrooms in the new house on Myrtle Way. At the rear, leading off the large open plan living area—it had large windows with a view over the hills, plenty of room for a couch, large coffee table, walls of bookshelves, a desk facing the window, a drafting board in the back corner, even a telescope.

It would be a highlight, for whomever ended up living there.

"Were you looking for something in particular?" Matt asked, cutting into an image Beau was building of *him* sitting at that desk, a blessed sense of calm coming over him as he looked out over that view. "Not that I'm rushing you."

"I was," said Beau. "I was…going to do some catching up."

"Okay," said Matt, his voice now a little giddy. "Want me to catch you up instead."

"Have at it."

Matt breathed out hard, then peppered Beau with bullet points, as if he'd been collecting them. The Luculent Engine had made it through phase one of independent testing. They were getting political blowback from the usual places, members who were sympathetic to fossil fuel providers. Another offer had been made for Lucky, double what they'd been offered last time.

"Tell them they're dreaming," Beau said.

And Matt laughed. Even though they were both pragmatic enough to know that leaking the story would give their rep as much of a boost as taking the money.

"How's the house coming?" Matt asked when he'd exhausted his bullet points.

"Come up and see."

"Is it still a bomb site?"

"Very much."

"Then not yet."

"Fair."

A beat of silence pulsed between them. One in which both wished to ask if the other was okay, both knowing the real answer was no…but improving. Whether they would improve in the same direction, Beau couldn't promise. Not yet.

"If you'd like to let my inbox off the leash, I'd be amenable," Beau said. And meant it. A week ago that would not have been possible. But now he could at least do that.

"I'd like that very much. Now prepare thyself for the deluge." With that, Matt hung up.

As threads of their conversation curled about inside his head—things said, things left out— Beau leaned back in the chair and the thing nearly toppled.

"The sooner the house is finished the better," he growled.

And Moose, thinking he was talking to him, nuzzled against his hand. Beau patted the dog back, while realising that Matt already knew something he'd not even considered.

In leaving, there had been a chance he might not go back at all.

Unlike Anushka Patel, most brides couldn't afford a wedding planner on top of the cost of everything else, so leaned on Charlie as a kind of "choose your own adventure" helper.

Some bought pre-negotiated packages such as attendance at three pre-wedding events, such as gift registry, first wedding-dress fitting, hens' breakfast, plus six phone calls, and twelve hours of pure bestie energy on the big day.

Others worked on hourly rates, calling on her when needed.

She even had a text message subscription service, via which brides could ask her anything, anytime, no question too small, no worry too trivial. It had been Julia's brilliant idea, her amazing bookkeeper-slash-backup-bridesmaid who'd been helping her set the thing up. And it was growing consistently, month on month. It was this last one that might even tide her over during the transition period when she left.

For example:

Q: My MOTHER IN-LAW did not disclose an ALLERGY to shellfish until today, THREE DAYS OUT from my wedding. In Hobart, on the water, with a full fresh-catch menu. What do I do?

A: First thing—breathe. Second thing—you're getting married in three days! Third thing—text me the details of the reception location, your caterer, and your MIL's favourite dinner. It will be sorted. Love, Always the Bridesmaid xxx

Of course, things didn't always go quite so swimmingly.

Charlie sat at her kitchen bench, staring at her laptop, while pressing fingers into her temples as she tried to block out the whir of concrete cutters coming from the house next door.

After the mega success of meeting Anushka and Bobby and their wedding party, she should have known karma would make amends. And it did, swiftly, using Isla the mega-introvert of the not-puce bridesmaid dresses as its vehicle.

"I'm not sure I can do this, Charlie," Isla had cried over the phone that morning.

"You can do anything. And anything you can't do, I'll do for you. Well, anything bar marry your guy."

Isla had laughed, then burst into a deeper set of sobbing tears.

"Okay," Charlie had said, "let's go back over the list we made of things we can do to make this not feel so terrifying."

"Well…" Isla sniffed.

"Well?" Charlie encouraged.

"There was one thing."

Elopement.

Apparently, after they'd rung off Isla had called Justin, he'd come straight home from work, they'd packed their bags and left to get married. Isla's mother-in-law had refused to pay the final Always the Bridesmaid invoice, and was threatening legal action to recoup the down payment.

As if she needed a sign of how precarious her situation really was, how careful she had to be, the light above Charlie's head crackled, flickered, and turned off. Then popped on again. Right as a piercingly high whine of construction equipment shook her window.

She could go over there and ask what time they might finish up so she could make some work calls without having to shout. But she'd done so a few days before, chocolate chip cookies in hand, only for Beau's project manager to stop her at the rose bushes.

They'd apparently been "told" not to let her through. "Unless you're in the appropriate safety gear," he said, accepting the cookies with a smile.

Charlie could have taken it as Beau trying to keep her safe, but her gut knew it was more than that.

He didn't want her there.

Since the roses had always been a rather pathetic excuse for a fence, he'd had to create an invisible way to make it clear that while they were working together, she no longer had unfettered access to his life.

As if his radio silence hadn't made that clear.

For after what had been an amazing night out, by all metrics, the only contact they'd had was her calendar updates regarding the Patel/Kent nuptials, and his thumbs-up. Which was *normal*, for people with a casual working relationship.

Only this was *Beau*. And so she couldn't let it lie.

He was upset with her, for pushing too hard about poor Milly. It must have been so difficult to speak about, and she'd pressed him till he felt he had no other choice.

Or it might have been the kiss.

Yes, it was on his cheek, and it had been a chaste thank-you kiss. But the way she'd leaned into him, the way her hand had curled into his shirt so that she'd had to tidy it up a little before stepping back... What had she been *thinking*?

She'd been *thinking* that she liked the way he looked at her these days. She'd been thinking that he was brilliant, and kind, and a little bit broken, and how that combination called to all the parts of her that had felt abandoned for so long. She'd been thinking that he had washed her dishes the other night without being asked.

She'd been *thinking* that for the first time in a

long time she felt at ease, happy, hopeful. And that having Beau Griffin in her life again, even for a short time, was turning out to be a little bit of magic.

She let her face fall into her hands, and tried really hard not to let the words *dumb* and *stupid* make their way through the whirr in her head.

Then, as the screech of the concrete cutter hummed to silence, someone next door turned on the radio, and the *Wicked* soundtrack began playing at full blast.

Without another thought, Charlie shot off the kitchen stool and out the back door. She got half-way across her yard, before she backtracked and grabbed a pair of yellow gum boots her mum used to wear when gardening, shucking them on as she made her way to Beau's.

When she pressed her way through the rose bushes there were no workmen to be seen out back. She heard the clang of a Ute tray closing in front of the house, an engine gunning, then the *Wicked* soundtrack softening as the truck left.

Meaning she stood in Beau's backyard, alone.

It had been a few days since the "chocolate chip cookie" debacle, a few days more since she'd found Beau there in lieu of the imaginary "rob-ber" and Moose had all but knocked her for six. And a lot had changed.

The yard had been cleaned up some. A flat patch graded in preparation for some kind of landscaping. The back facade had been painted a lovely warm cream. And the glass had gone in downstairs—an entire wall of it in soft smoky grey that reflected the view beyond.

"*Oh*," she said, the delighted sound coming out before she could stop it. While for some time the place had looked so imposing, so hard, she could see how it might, in the end, reflect, enhance, and become one with the land around it. Not fighting it, or taming it, but existing together. Each bringing out the best in the other.

And her head of steam dissipated as if a cold change had swept over the valley.

"Charlie?"

Wincing at having been caught trespassing, Charlie turned to find Beau picking his way down the side of the house in a T-shirt, old jeans, work boots, and his ubiquitous hard hat. He had a smear of dirt on his neck, a graze in the knee of his jeans, and sweat patches all over his shirt, the fabric clinging to him in a way that turned her mouth dry.

"I came to ask your guys if they might turn the music down a smidge, but either my timing was excellent or I scared them off."

"Not a fan of *Wicked*?" he asked, with no hint of all the tumult she'd spent the past few days imagining him roiling in.

In fact, he looked chipper. Healthy. Refreshed. All the more gorgeous for it.

"Are you kidding?" she said, dragging her mind back to the subject at hand. She belted out a few terrible notes of "Popular." "I'm just not sure it goes all that well with a concrete-cutter accompaniment!"

He smiled. And did it just reach his eyes? Yes! There was a definite glint in those warm, autumn leaf depths. Her heart did a happy little jig against her ribs, till she told it to calm the heck down.

Which was never going to happen when Beau suddenly seemed to clock the "outfit" she'd grabbed off her clean clothes chair after her shower that morning, knowing she'd be working from home—a Miss Piggy tank top, frill pink gingham cotton pyjama shorts, and once-yellow gum boots.

He gave her outfit the quickest possible up and down, and yet she felt as if he'd run his hands over every inch of her skin his gaze had touched. And when that gaze once again met hers, he looked at her in a way that meant, when she got home, she'd be putting her head in the freezer.

"I freaked you out the other night," she blurted.

He stilled, then used the back of his hand to wipe a bead of sweat from his brow. And said nothing, because he was a listener and she was a talker, meaning she had no choice but to follow through.

"By kissing you. Twice. On the cheek, yes, but still that must have felt as if it came out of nowhere. Even though it didn't, because I am so grateful for what you're doing for me. Then I pushed you into telling me about Milly, when I'm sure that was never your intention. And I want to apologise for both."

He lowered his hand to his hip, grit coating the creases in his knuckles. Stylish guy Beau was quite the thing, but manual labour Beau was making her knees turn to liquid.

"You have nothing to apologise for, Charlie. In fact, it unblocked something inside me."

"The kiss?"

He tilted his head in a manner that felt wholly indulgent, and her dry mouth felt so parched she had to swallow, hard.

"The conversation," he said, his voice hitting a deeper note. "I've been feeling a lot of feelings, and had nowhere to put them. Not wanting to bother Matt, and not ready to talk to a stranger about it all."

"And I'm neither!" she said, her voice bright.

"You are most definitely neither. So, while it wasn't my intention, it helped."

"I'm…glad." Understatement alert. For she was quietly giddy. First that she'd *not* screwed things up, also that she'd actually been a force for good. She really was getting her mojo back!

As to who she was to Beau now? Neither of them, it seemed, was in any place to fill that blank space.

Beau smiled. "While you're here, do you want a tour?"

"Sure," she said, curiosity piqued. Then looked around. "No Moose?"

"Left him at the rental with something called a Kong? Filled with peanut butter. The local grocer recommended it when he saw how much dog food I was buying."

"Phil! Isn't he the sweetest? He was my backup if you said no."

Beau, clearly picturing Phil on his special stool behind the counter, his one working hearing aid, his tufty silver hair, deadpanned her. "Is that right?"

"Mm-hmm," she said, the picture of innocence, marvelling at how light she felt, when five minutes earlier she'd been all rain clouds. "Now show me around."

Only Beau glanced at the top of her head, which still in its messy shower bun was, of course, "hard hat" free. And she deflated like a nicked balloon.

Beau held up a hand, "Can you... Just wait here a sec." Then he held out a second hand, doubling down, untrusting that she'd not follow.

Charlie threw her hands out to the side as she watched him step over rocks and old bricks and disappear back around the side of the house.

When he returned, he held a large black gift bag.

"For me?" she asked, when he held it out to her.

Beau nodded, eyes gleaming behind his adorably smudged glasses.

Flutters of anticipation and surprise dancing inside her, Charlie looked into the bag to find...

A hard hat. In a bright pale peach. And her heart squeezed so hard she had to let out a breath.

Slipping the hat from the bag, she looked to Beau. Speechless for once in her life.

"So, you can come over anytime," he explained, "to stickybeak, or bring the guys baked goods, or put in requests if you prefer *Hamilton*, or *The Muppets*," he said, with a quick flicker of his eyes to her top. "And so that I can sleep better at night."

He'd been thinking about her, when not with her. Worrying, even. And while there were a thousand ways she could have brushed it off, made a joke, lightened the sweet tension curling inside her, she couldn't. Even while it was so unusual for *her* to be the one being looked after, and it felt disorienting as all hell.

Because now she knew about his grief. The shadow trapped inside him that surely touched all other areas of his life. Including her. Meaning she had to take extra care.

So she pulled the hat from the bag and sat it on her head, with a, "Ta da!"

"May I?" Beau asked, then moved in close to shift the hat so it sat more firmly on her head. "There. Better."

When his eyes dropped back to hers, he blinked.

He looked from one eye to the other, as if trying to read whatever was written there. Then his gaze dropped to her mouth. And stayed.

The urge to lick her lips was agonising, but she didn't want him to get the wrong idea. Or the right idea. That she'd been thinking about him when she wasn't with him, too.

Because what good would that do?

"Now I'm properly decked out, are you going to give me the grand tour or not?" she said, a small miracle the words came out at all.

Beau nodded, and blinked furiously, his jaw tight, his cheeks a little pink. Then he held out at an arm, and said, "After you."

Rolling her eyes at the sky, and muttering to herself to keep it together, Charlie picked her way around piles of detritus to look through the downstairs glass.

"It'll remain open-plan," he said, moving in beside her, but not too close. Which was fine with her. "There'll be a kitchenette at the rear, bathroom, so it might be a granny flat, or office space. Options."

Options for whom? she suddenly wanted to know. Needed to know with a ferocity that surprised even her. But after the strange tension of the past few minutes, she decided not to press.

Next he pointed out space for the wine cellar, and a laundry/mudroom. The foundation for the ice bath. Sauna. Gym.

"No dungeon?" she asked, lifting up onto her toes as if she might then find a secret trap door.

"We tried, but the foundations were too hard."

"Don't you hate that?" Then, as she'd held off as long as she could, she said, "A gym is a pretty nice add on for a holiday place. Or a rental. Unless…unless you plan to sell the place?"

Despite his family having not owned it for the past decade, that felt wrong somehow. As if, in some secret place inside her, after Beau had left, and while she'd been overseas, she'd taken some small comfort in the Griffins and the Goodes being connected by their rose bushes still.

Then Beau lifted a hand to his neck and said, "When I set to knocking the old place down and building anew, that was the part I focused on most of all."

"And now?"

His gaze met hers, the muscles in his raised arm bunching. "Now I'm not sure. The closer it gets, the less I like the idea of other people getting the benefit of what we're building here. At least at first."

"So, at the end of the build, a few weeks from now, you might stay on?"

Stop! Her inner monologue woke up. *Stop pushing him. What he does with the place is none of your business. If all goes well, a few weeks from now you can pack your bags and flee! So leave the man alone.*

Then Beau breathed in, his gaze still locked on hers. "I don't know. Maybe."

"Hmm," she said, her breath light. "I mean, you could. But keep in mind the Wi-Fi signal is touch and go. Everything *city* is a good hour's drive away, at least. Then there's your very fancy, very important, very well-paying job, which happens to be in Sydney, meaning it'd be a hell of a commute. And—"

I won't be here.

Charlie gulped. Chuffed she'd managed to cut herself off before blurting out that last part. For she had nothing to do with his reasons to stay, or to go. Just as he had nothing to do with hers. If their being here at the same time had a purpose, surely it was to find some kind of closure.

"And I'm *not* sure that tearing down your parents' house and building something in its place actually wipes out the horrors that happened here."

Beau's arm dropped, and he looked up at the mighty house looming over them. "While I'm not sure that living in a museum dedicated to the worst of your childhood is any better."

Charlie's jaw dropped. "Wow, burn."

His gaze moved back to her, eyebrows raised. "Am I wrong?"

"For one thing, as soon as I can afford to get out of here, I will."

"Is that so?"

"Yes," she shot back. "It is entirely so. It's *why* Anushka and Bobby's wedding was important enough for me to rope you into the thing. And *why* making myself at home here hasn't been a priority."

"Mmm," he said, so noncommittal she ached to press back.

Instead, rolling out her shoulder, Charlie glanced over the rose bushes to the familiar skyline of the house next door. The house that carried the echoes of her father in the bookshelves in the sunroom, the jackets in his bedroom cupboard, his office, completely untouched. While the vegetable and herb gardens that had been her mother's salvation had been reclaimed by the earth.

And all the arguments she felt backing up in her throat turned to dust.

She let her face fall into her hands. Then remembered the hard hat, righting it as it began to slip. "Aren't we the pair?"

"What's the saying—wherever you go, there you are."

"Isn't that the truth?"

After a few long moments, Beau said, "It wasn't entirely horrible." And she knew he meant his childhood, because of her.

She moved a little closer and bumped him with her shoulder.

And he bumped her back.

"As for this house," she said, moving out from under the cantilevered balcony and into the yard, where she might be able to find air not infused with his warmth, his scent. "I may have been a tad disparaging at first. For it's definitely less like a weapons facility than I first imagined."

Beau, who had followed, gave her a warm smile.

"Great! Okay! Well, I have stuff to do, so if you could let your guys know to keep the radio down a decibel or two, that'd be great."

"Will do."

She took a step back, and tripped off the edge of the balcony foundation. Beau reached for her, but she righted herself just fine.

She pointed at him as she backed away. "If the next time I come over you have a roll of bubble wrap fashioned into overalls, that's where I draw the line."

He held up both hands, palms out.

After which, she turned and clomped back to hers.

And if she put the hard hat in a special place on the corner of the kitchen bench, then so be it.

CHAPTER SEVEN

IN BETWEEN BEAU'S suit try-ons and lunch in Noosa with Anushka and her soon to be mother-in-law at the fancy restaurant of the chef who was catering the event, she had back-to-back weddings with other clients on the weekends.

Keeping Robin's handsy cousin Stu occupied—a cinch. Keeping Gladys's tipsy Pastor Ron away from the punch before the backyard wedding—not as easy, but done. Each bride sent off happy, and relieved all had gone well.

High on her run of success, and a little on the fact that so far none of Anushka's circle had looked at her and said, "Hey didn't you throw cake at a bride once?", on the next cool free afternoon Charlie took a trip into town to pick up fertiliser, seedlings, seeds, mulch, and a few gardening tools.

For the frames of her mother's veggie and herb gardens were still there, and the thought of bringing them back to life that had been seeded by Beau's rather pointed comment about how she was living in a morbid museum had grown with each passing day.

Sure, it might not eventuate by the time she left, she might not get to reap the benefits, but in the same way Beau was leaving his mark on the house next door, she wanted to sprinkle her brand of joy on this place, too.

It was near dark by the time she'd softened up the soil, weeded the beds, added soil, watered, and planted a few seeds. Just enough light to stand back and take some photos to send to her mum. Who'd sent her back an eggplant emoji, which Charlie could only hope referred to the veggie garden.

A cool breeze swept in from the valley, as Charlie cricked her back. Looking out over the view, to where the moon gleamed down on the distant water, Charlie saw the first stars twinkling in the sky.

Feeling loose and warm and rather pleased with herself, she washed her hands, grabbed a throw, spread it out on the back lawn and lay down on her back, watching as the sky went from mauve to deep blue to black.

It was pure muscle memory that had set her down in the exact spot she and Beau used to do exactly this. Sneaking outside at some ungodly hour, long after their parents had fallen asleep, ostensibly to count shooting stars. But mostly to talk about school, about how they imagined their futures might be. Knowing, from experience, the next day would be better for it.

The rustle of the rose bushes, followed by Moose's doggy snuffle were the first signs she was about to have a visitor, the vibration of Beau's heavy boots on the ground as he neared was the next.

"Boots off," she said, "hard hat, too, if you're wearing it. This is a safety-free zone."

She saw him pause, out of the corner of her eye, before doing as he asked. Then Moose's face filled her vision as he licked at her chin. Laughing, she patted the ground beside her, and after a few turns in the soft unmown grass, Moose lay down with a *harrumph*.

"Where have you gone?" she asked, then looked overhead to find him staring at her back porch, the light above it so weak she'd not even bothered to turn it off. "You are obsessed with that thing. I will get to it. It's on a long list of exciting DIY projects I have decided to take on."

He looked back at her, and even upside down, and frowning; he made for a fine view.

She went back to looking up at the stars.

"I'm assuming the other half of that blanket is for me," said Beau as he neared.

Had she deliberately lain on one side, just in case he found her there? She'd known he'd been about, had seen him head down into the drop at the edge of his backyard, garden sheers in hand, as if he was going to attempt to tackle the lantana himself.

"Whoever calls dibs," she said.

With a soft laugh, Beau dropped to the blanket beside her. She felt the heat of him, the bulk, shift the air around her as he laid his big body down. He smelled of hard work, dirt, and botanicals. And something other that she was beginning to recognise as pure Beau.

"Remind me of the rules," he said, and a frisson of delight sparked inside her, that he remembered this had been their thing, too.

"We can't leave till we've both seen a shooting star."

"Found any?" he asked.

"Not yet."

And after a few quiet minutes spent revelling in the brush of the wind, the hum of distant frog song, it became dark enough that if she squinted just right, she could just make out the pale ribbon of the Milky Way.

"You won't see *that* in the city," he said. Convincing himself it was a plus of living here, *staying* here, or convincing her?

"Do you remember the time, we were around fourteen, when you tried telling me that shooting stars weren't stars at all, that they were big rocks, or space junk, burning up as they entered Earth's atmosphere?"

"Because it's the truth."

Charlie laughed, the press of it hard against her ribs. "But not the *point*."

"What was the point?"

This, she thought. *Us being together.*

"The point, dear Beau, was the beauty and ferocity and vastness of the universe making our problems seem a little less all-consuming."

"Mmm," he said, his voice a growl in the darkness, and Charlie's skin raised in goose bumps.

"So, I hear you had lunch with Bobby this week."

"I did. Hope that's okay?"

"Of course! Outside of my needs, you do you, boo."

Anushka had called Charlie to gush over how Bobby had a total boy crush on Beau and wasn't that the sweetest thing ever. And Charlie had wholeheartedly agreed, while also having to stave off a raging case of pride that Beau was out there, making friends and doing nice things for himself. As if the depression/bargaining might be easing up some. And it was her doing.

"And am I meeting your needs?"

Her needs?

Oh, he meant regarding the gig! "Yep. Sure. You're doing great. I'll let you know if you're not, don't worry about that."

"Okay." Then, "How long does this usually take?"

"To see a shooting star? Why so impatient?"

He moved around beside her, his foot knocking against hers, sending what felt like a belt of shooting stars up her leg. "I've been pushing Sisyphus's rock up a hill all afternoon, trying to clear out the scrub out back, and if I lie here too long my back will seize up and I'll be walking funny tomorrow."

Laughing, Charlie pulled herself to sitting, and Beau did the same.

She looked sideways to find him watching her, not the sky. "I could have told you that you need a pro to clear lantana."

"You knew I was out there. I saw you watching."

Oops.

Had his voice dropped a little as he asked, "So why didn't you tell me?"

The answer—because then she'd have missed out on watching him walk up and down the hill, getting sweatier and messier as the day went on.

"Most of the men I've known haven't appreciated my advice, or opinions, or skill set when it came to such things."

Beau took that in. "Then most of the men you've known were fools."

She leaned back on her hands, let her legs stretch out in front. And said, "True that."

Beau, after watching her for a few heady moments, did the same. His bare foot brushing hers. She knocked it back. And once they'd settled, their little toes touched, though neither said a thing about it.

"You've mentioned a few times now that you're keen to head off," he said.

"As soon as humanly possible." Though it had been her mantra for months, this time it felt a little hollow.

"Then why come back at all?"

Whether it was the cloak of darkness, or mention of the men she'd known, or the fact that this was the place they'd talked about their big fears, she found herself telling Beau about #cakegate.

Her heart was thudding in her ears by the time she got to the moment Richard had slunk in behind her. Leaving out his choice words, she jumped to when she came out of a fog to find she'd thrown cake across the room. And yet, in reliving it, she felt as if she was back there, right in the middle of it, Richard's gaze bright with shocked delight.

"Does any of that ring a bell?" she asked.

Beau, watching her in that quiet way of his, shook his head.

So Charlie grabbed her phone from where she'd sat it on the edge of the throw, googled, and pages of images glowed brightly on the screen. She scrolled down till she found the infamous video.

The vision was shaky, zoomed in from the back of the large room. Heads bobbing in and out of view, focus shifting before the bright pink castle cake came into view.

"Phones had been forbidden," she said, "left in baskets at the door, as the rights had been sold to an online wedding site. But naturally someone had not complied. Meaning the only footage is this. After Richard had thrown his bride in front of him."

She watched Beau's face rather than the video, not needing to see it to know exactly which part it was up to. His expression remained impassive, until the security escorted her from the venue, at which point his nostrils flared and his gaze shot to her.

"What the hell did he do?" Beau asked.

"Hmm?"

"The groom. He said something. Or did something. It wasn't just that he was there. I know you, Charlie. You've faced down monsters with phenomenal grace your whole life. What did he do?"

Charlie swallowed. Tried to brush it off, the way she had in those first few months. Until a need to get it out of her, like an exorcism, had the words spilling from her mouth.

Beau's jaw grew tight, his eyes fierce behind his glasses, as she told him what Richard had said. How he'd called her a screwup. And far worse. In her place of business, where she'd worked so hard to build herself up into something more. Until she'd snapped.

"Wait," he said. "Did no one stop to ask why? Did no one assume you had good reason to do what you did?"

Charlie blinked. "Ah, no." In fact, it had never once occurred to her that they should. "He's an asshole, yes. But I still should never have done what I did. The worst part—it was reactive and dramatic and utter self-sabotage. Everything my father always accused me of being. I remember feeling as if he was watching. Feeling as I was screaming, in my head, *See! You were right!* And now it's going to follow me my entire life."

She turned her phone toward herself and turned off the screen.

While Beau looked out at the distant sky.

Having told her side, fully, for the first time since the whole thing began, she felt terrible, and relieved, in equal measure.

Whatever happened from here would happen. So long as he didn't say he could now no longer go ahead with the wedding, anything else she could handle. She hoped.

Then, voice low with a note of feral that had her insides curling, he said, "Where does he live? What's he most afraid of? Any allergies? I'll sort him out."

And she laughed. A quick bark, then more. Guffaws that brought tears to her eyes. Tears she'd not cried at the time, her entire body rigid with shock.

Then, when she was done, she looked at him.

"He doesn't matter," she said, and found that she meant it. Lately she was beginning to see the difference. "Karma will get him in the end. While look at me! The mistress of my own domain. Sure, the electrics are shot, and I walked down the hall this morning and I felt as if I was tipping sideways, meaning the place probably needs to be restumped. I've dropped every cent I've made so far with Always the Bridesmaid in keeping it from falling on my head. But it's better, not being there. Not being that... Charlotte. Stripped back I've had to be...me."

"From my point of view, there's nothing at all wrong with that."

She smiled. Then looked up at the sky. Because if she looked at Beau, the way he was looking at her, she might just cry.

A minute later Beau said, "There."

Charlie leaned in and followed the point of his finger to catch the tail end of a bright shooting star, shimmering back to darkness. Then she laughed, the joy of it fizzing her. "It never gets old, does it?"

"No," he said, "it seems it does not."

When she turned to smile at him, his face was tipped to hers. They were so close, their noses nearly touched. And the heat in his eyes was so patent he felt it hit her cheeks in a warm glow.

Then he reached for her, his hand hovering near

her cheek. When she didn't demur, his fingers moved to tuck her hair behind her ear.

Alarm bells sounded. A riotous clang.

Don't do this. He's hurting. He's confused. He's breaking things and remaking things and isn't entirely sure why. Things are finally kind of okay. Don't mess things up.

Or perhaps they were celebratory bells. A rousing cheer going up inside her. That after being separated by oceans, and time, having lived lives that had challenged and forged them in new ways, they'd found their way back here. To one another. For the shortest of times, before the universe was set to fling them apart again, but still.

Then, as Beau breathed her in, his gaze roving over her face, his fingers on her skin, she knew it wasn't closure she'd been yearning for since the moment he knocked on her door.

It was this.

Charlie lifted her head and his hand moved with it, now cupping her jaw, his thumb moving to trace her cheekbone, the edge of her mouth. His gaze followed, drinking her in, taking his fill. As if he, too, felt the press of time.

Where he touched her, she burned. Where he didn't, she ached. And when his gaze found hers, his mouth curved into an understanding smile.

She lifted her hand to his face, her fingers sliding against his jaw, the rough stubble sending splinters of electricity down her arm. And a small moan escaped the back of his throat.

He touched her with such tenderness, and such restraint, it was too much. And not enough. She felt like she was floating, and tipped her forehead to his in order not to float away.

Then, finding a note of bravery, she might not have had had she not told him her truth, if he'd not given her reason to trust him with it, Charlie lifted her head and pressed her lips to his.

A kiss.

She was kissing Beau Griffin. Something she'd dreamed of more times than she dared count. Pining for him, confused by him, missing him.

It was the lightest of things—a brush of lips. Then another. All the while time seemed to stand still. Her blood turning sluggish, as her fingers traced his jaw before delving into his thick hair. Touching him, learning him, committing him to memory lest she wake to find this was a dream, too.

And the kiss. Oh, the kiss!

It was slow, delicate. A gentle touch and release as they learned one another's shape, warmth, feel, taste. Like a flower that blossoms once a year right on midnight, utterly precious, utterly wondrous.

But she knew it could be more.

Needing to be closer, to wrap herself in him, she moved up onto her knees. In complete sync,

Beau's arm gathered her around the waist hauling her over him, so that she straddled him. Her hand slid up his back, under his shirt, the sheen of sweat and hot skin and steely strength made her weak.

But he had her. Gathered her to him, holding her close, her body curled against his. All movement, and rolling bodies. And sliding touch.

Then his tongue traced the seam of her lips, opening her to him, and everything changed. The world went dark, and light, and sweet, and lush. Heat rolled through her in waves as her body turned both limp with need and as light as if it was full of sparkles.

Then Beau breathed out, her name a whisper against her lips. An ode. An incantation. As he kissed his way along her jaw. Her head fell back as he pressed sweet drugging kisses to her neck.

The words he was saying, words of want, and heat, and need, melted together till she no longer heard them, only felt them. A rising tide of lust inside her, burning her alive.

Then a loud *woof* broke through the fog, and another, and Beau's lips paused at the edge of her top. One hand in her hair, the other hooked under the strap of her bra.

Charlie opened her eyes to find herself on her knees, Beau's hard thighs beneath her, her head back, the stars a glittering spray across the sky.

She stayed a beat, trying to find her centre,

before she slowly dropped her head to find Beau breathing deep, his lips damp, his eyes diamond bright.

Then Moose huffed a breath in their faces, and they disentangled quickly, as Moose woofed around the stick in his mouth.

Beau reached out and grabbed the thing, wincing at the slobber on his hand, before he tossed the thing across the yard.

"Saved by the dog?" he murmured and Charlie laughed.

While she'd been thinking what a fine thing it might have been if this was a day he'd left the lovely Moose at home.

But no. This was better.

A kiss was wild enough. A kiss wasn't *that* big a deal. People did it all the time!

In fact, maybe it had been inevitable. All that history, and Beau going through what he was going through, and Charlie with the whole Richard and #cakegate debacle. It was a lot. A kiss might take the edge off, without completely messing with the nice thing they had.

She glanced to Beau, who was running his hands through his hair. His brow furrowed as if he, too, was thinking hard. Then he heaved himself to standing, all athletic grace for a man his size. It was enough to set her heart to racing again. When he looked down at her, he let out a great sigh, before holding out a hand to help her up.

As she took it, her breath leaving her as he lifted her to her feet, she cried, "Look!" as a spectacular shooting star curved to life behind his shoulder, perhaps the best she'd ever seen, its tail a blinding mix of colour across the sky.

Magic in the air, and hormones still raging through her body, for a second Charlie considered asking Beau to stay. For dinner. And then?

Beau said, "Well, we've both spotted a shooting star; rules say it's time for me to leave."

And she swallowed her invitation back. "You always did have a thing for the rules."

And yet there they stood, for a few long seconds, as if there was too much to say, but neither knew where to begin. Then, when Moose came bounding back with his stick, Beau started walking backward toward the rose bushes.

"Don't forget, you have another suit fitting next week," Charlie called.

"I won't forget," he said, still walking backward, as if he wasn't quite ready to see her face for the last time that night.

Which was how Charlie felt herself blurting, "I have a wedding on this weekend. Quite a cool one in fact. Takes place on a train. And I have a standing plus-one, if you'd like to come?"

Beau paused. Taking his time answering. Oh, no, he was looking for some way to let her down, wasn't he? Concerned she thought the kiss meant something more than what it was.

"Think of it as a dry run," she said. "So you can see what it is that I do on the day," she added, wishing she'd led with that.

"Fine," he said, his voice cavernous in the darkness.

And for the first time she wished both her back lights were working so she could see his face. See if he looked pained, or if he was smiling that half smile. See if the light reached his eyes.

Then she was glad of the darkness when she remembered, "It's an overnighter. Do you have anyone who can look after Moose?"

"I have someone."

"Great! Saturday morning. Wear a suit. Pack an overnight bag. Pick me up at ten a.m. in the sexy rocket car?"

Beau's laughter danced across the darkness and Charlie crossed her arms, holding it close.

"See you then, Charlie," Beau said, then he and his dog were gone.

CHAPTER EIGHT

BEAU LEANED AGAINST the bar, the glass in his hand only three quarters full in consideration of the rocking of the train.

While around him wedding guests guzzled and nibbled and got generally sozzled, as the grandly appointed carriage shuttled them south to where they would soon all disembark, witness the wedding, then hop back on the train where the real party started.

At least that's how Charlie had described the order of ceremony, before she'd ducked away to look after her client, Ginny, leaving him with nothing to do to distract him from thoughts of her.

For that's where his thoughts had lived since their evening star gaze, tipping from the sweet salty taste of her, the heat of her skin, the way she curled into him with such abandon to incredulity as to the events that had sent her careening back home. His equilibrium up the spout.

After spending months feeling little but apathy, he now had a surfeit of energy to deal with. He had to put it somewhere. That somewhere turned out to be poring through applications for future works plans as submitted by Luculent's junior engineers. Making sure to support those to whom he was obligated, where in Charlie's case that had not happened at all.

His phone buzzed. His blood heated, thinking it might be her. Instead, he was blessed with a photo of Mike, the electrician, sitting beside Moose on his couch, watching *Turner and Hooch.*

Beau downed his iced water, the last thing Charlie needed was her date getting tipsy, and ordered another. Not that he was her *date.* He was shadowing her, learning from the master, in readiness for Anushka and Bobby's wedding in three short weeks. For all that his role would be a one-time gig, he found himself truly curious to see how it all went down.

An hour later, as the well-lubricated guests poured from the train and onto the platform where the wedding was to take place, Beau took up a spot at the rear, meaning he was in prime position to see the wedding party's big entrance.

But all he saw was Charlie. Her dress appeared more sparkles than fabric, her hair in slick waves, her lips a dark luscious pink; she looked ready to tempt a mobster to go straight. Or a priest to turn rogue.

Her confident gaze swept over the crowd, as if

making sure they were all behaving, until it found him. And there it stayed.

He felt his heart buck against his ribs, his skin felt a little tight, and his extremities began to cool as if all his blood had rushed somewhere more important.

He lifted a hand to his heart, intimating an arrow had hit, right there. It earned him a twist of a smile, and the most subtle of eye rolls, before she slid her eyes back to the front and for the next several hours, gave everything she had to her bride.

Once they were back in the bar carriage, she slid through the room like silk—passing out tissues, sneaking away drinks from those who'd had their share, keeping the fathers of bride and groom—whom Beau had been told did not get on—laughing and relaxed. It was no surprise, having been the original receiver of her fixed attentions as a kid, yet watching from the outside, she was a sensation.

When she caught his eye late into the night, he lifted his drink in salute. She motioned to see if he needed her and he shook his head. After a beat, she excused herself and made her way through the crowd toward him.

"I'm parched," she said as she slid into the gap he made.

The waiter slid her the iced water Beau had just ordered for her.

"Wow. You're a natural. If you ever wanted to give up playing with cars for a living, being at my beck and call might be a great backup option."

He lifted his glass, clinked it against hers, and they watched one another as they drank. He wondered if he looked as flushed as she did. If his pupils were as large. If she could see the same thoughts in his eyes that he could see in hers.

"Have you picked up any ideas?" she asked. "For when it's your turn?"

"The best man stands beside the…bride, right?"

She laughed, then glared. Then, sighing, looked around, as if she'd not yet had the chance. "This is pretty amazing, don't you think?"

"It really is."

The carriage was packed, a three-piece band played '90s boy band songs in a classical manner at the far end, and everyone rocked in gentle tandem with the movement of the train.

When she looked up at him again, it was like some magnetic force was drawing them both there. Beau felt a *boom-boom-boom* behind his ribs, as if a gong had been struck.

Then something caught her eye across the bar, and she winced. "Sorry, gotta go."

But then, after a beat, she tipped up onto her toes, slid her hand along the back of his neck and kissed him. Hard. When she pulled away, Beau leaned in, chasing her mouth, to kiss her again. Softer this time, a tender promise.

"Marking my place," he said, before she sighed, then disappeared into the crowd.

Only for the *boom-boom-boom* to continue. Like a drumbeat. A harbinger.

No, like a ticking clock.

Hours later, once the wedding guests had retired to their sleeper cars, Ginny—eyes rimmed in watery kohl, lipstick long gone—pulled Charlie into a hard hug.

"You are a professional angel," Ginny said.

"I'm better than that. I'm a professional bestie."

Ginny's eyes widened. "OMG, that's exactly what you are. Whereas your guy, he's a professional sweetheart. My dad loves him. Maybe more than he loves Callum."

"Okay, time for bed."

"I will never forget this. I will never forget you."

Charlie, who was pragmatic enough to know that her part in Ginny's story was a mere heartbeat, peeled Ginny's grip from her arm, and transferred it to her husband's. Callum, for whom this was clearly nothing new, mouthed *thank you*, before guiding his happy teary bride to their wedding suite.

Then with a huge sigh, she turned to Beau who was sitting in a booth, checking his phone. He turned it around to show her a photo of Moose asleep on Mike the electrician's bed.

"I'm going to regret this," he said, "aren't I?"

Charlie, who'd been counting down the minutes since Beau had marked his place, shrugged. "Oh, I don't know. It's been a pretty good night so far."

Beau slowly lowered his phone, before peeling himself out from behind the table. He stood before her, looking like a million dollars in what had to be a custom suit, the way it made the absolute most of every glorious piece of him. This long tall drink of heaven.

The lights dimmed, a sign they were the last ones left. And Charlie yawned, then rocked on her feet in a way that had nothing to do with the train.

Beau laughed softly. "Come on, Sleeping Beauty. Time to get you to bed, before you collapse on the floor."

Then he held out his hand, and when she placed hers there, he entwined his fingers with hers. Then led her out of the bar carriage and down the gently swaying hall past the sleepers till she found their room number.

When she pulled her key from her clutch, Beau was standing danger close. She could sense his breaths, feel his pulse. Her own heart was beating like crazy by the time she managed to open the door to find a big, neat double bed looking back at her.

She slammed the door shut, and turned to block the way.

"Is there a problem?" Beau asked.

"No. Yes. Sorry. I was told I'd been given a twin

room, in case it turned out I needed an assistant for such an unusual job."

"Charlie," Beau said, gently moving her to one side. Then he opened the door. After a beat he said, "That's our luggage against the wall, so I guess this is our room."

He moved inside so she had no choice but to follow.

"There are semi-recliners, halfway down the train," she said. "I've slept in stranger places than that, so I'm more than happy to take one for the team."

Beau turned, the room getting smaller just by him being in it. "Charlie."

She swallowed. "I just don't want you to think that I invited you along to…" She glanced at the bed.

"I hadn't thought as much, but the more you point it out, the more of an elephant in the room it seems to become."

"Right." Good point. "So do you want first shower?"

"You look like you're about to fall asleep where you stand, so you go first."

Great. She was vibrating with memories of his kiss, and visions of the bed before her, and in his eyes she looked tired.

She went to give her zip a head start. Reaching with her right hand, then her left, only to find the tag was tucked in too deep.

When she growled in frustration, Beau asked, "Are you okay?"

"Yep." She tried twisting the neck a little toward the front. No luck there, either. She breathed out, exhaustion creeping up on her fast. "Do you mind?"

Beau looked at her a moment, his nostrils flaring, his eyes dark behind his glasses, before he gave her a short nod.

She turned, and moved her hair out of the way. When Beau's hands touched the back of her neck, she shivered. Enough that he waited a moment, before his fingers found the zipper tag and slid it down, slowly, so that she could feel the warmth of his fingers curling down her spine.

When his fingers hit her lower spine, her dress fell forward. She gathered it at her front, and turned to send him a quick thank-you, only to find him already moving around to the other side of the bed.

He stood facing the window for a long moment, his hands on his hips, his body taut, before he rid himself of his jacket and removed his cufflinks with such spare elegance her heart hurt.

"Ginny wanted me to pass on her thanks for the time you spent with her dad," Charlie said.

Beau stopped, his shoulder turning slightly, but his face remained turned away. "Turns out Ginny's dad is the reason we are here, for he is a train spotter. I now know all there is to know about every train that ever was."

Charlie winced. "You weren't on the clock. You didn't have to do that."

"Did it help you?"

"*Me?* Well, yes actually."

"Then that's *all* there is to know."

Charlie hadn't invited him to come, expecting anything to happen. She'd just wanted to be with him. As often as she could, before their time ran out. Then, the entire day, knowing he was near, she'd felt as if her blood was filled with bubbles.

And now, knowing he'd put himself out for no reason but to make her day easier, knowing how he kissed, how often she felt his eyes on her through the day, she couldn't remember why she was making this so hard.

Before she could think herself around in another circle, she let her dress fall forward, the shimmering fabric landing in a heavy *swish* at her feet. By the way Beau's shoulders tensed, the way he stood rock still, she knew he'd heard.

Then he looked up, his gaze catching hers in the reflection in the train window.

Time seemed to pause, as if teetering between their past and future. A crux on which everything would change. Irrevocably. Forever.

Beau turned, slowly. His jaw was like granite, his eyes crystal bright, as he took her in. Naked bar a fine beige G-string and silver high heels.

"Charlotte," he said, his voice cavernous, and she didn't correct him. For hearing her name, in that voice, it felt like a promise.

He was too far away, all the way over on the other side of the bed. So she knelt on the edge, and crawled her way to him. Which had seemed like a good idea at the time, as she'd not expected the mattress to be so soft.

When she reached him, she lifted onto her knees and instantly toppled forward. Thankfully, he came out of his fog in time to catch her.

He gathered her to him, his arms around her back, while her hands pressed against his chest. She felt the steady beat of his heart. Felt his strength, and his restraint. Breathed in to find he smelled like a woodland grove and some deeply masculine note that made her head go woozy.

"Earlier," he said, his eyes determinedly on hers, rather than all the naked skin below. "Earlier, when I said that I was marking my place, that was not with any expectation—"

"Do you want to kiss me again, Beau?"

His hands slid up her back, gathering her hair at the nape of her neck. While his body, hard, and ready for her, pressed against her chest. And she wasn't sure he had a clue either thing was happening.

"I do," he said. "I want to kiss you more than I need air."

"Then kiss me," she said.

He didn't need to be asked twice.

With a growl he ducked his head and pressed his mouth to hers. No gentle exploration this time. Where their first kiss had been soft, and sweet, and like fresh honey and starlight, this was pure fire.

His tongue swept into her open mouth as they shared lush open-mouthed kisses. Her hands were in his hair, his arms hauling her close. Bodies pressed together, as if they could not get close enough.

Then he let her fall back a little, enough that she gasped, as he slid an arm behind her knees, then lifted her into his arms. It was a hell of a move. Made even more impressive when he turned and lowered her to the bed, before lowering himself over her.

She grabbed him by the back of the head and kissed him. And kissed him. And kissed him.

Until she was no longer inside her own body. She was a kiss. She was roving hands and delicate sighs and limbs curled over limbs. She was rising heat, and liquid pleasure.

Then he shifted, his thigh pressing between hers, and she broke the kiss to gasp. Sucking in breath, her eyes shut tight as she bore down into the sensation. Her blood was so high, her nerves so wrought, she felt like she could come at any moment.

As if he knew it, as if he could read her every

breath, every gasp, the way she tugged at his hair, and writhed beneath him, Beau pulled back. An inch, enough. And her eyes fluttered open.

No, come back, she thought, and shifted down the bed, reaching for his backside, still clad in suit pants. How was he still dressed when she was all skin and heat?

He laughed, then moaned as he pinned her to the spot. When she growled at him, he silenced her with a kiss. A kiss so sweet, and deft, and perfect she melted into the bed.

"There's no rush."

But there was. She could feel it. Time slipping away. His house, Anushka's wedding, her freedom.

"Speak for yourself," she said. Taking his moment of distraction to let her knees fall out to the sides. He sank against her, a hiss leaving his mouth, as he nestled into the cradle she'd created, a perfect fit.

He lifted a hand then, and brushed her hair from her face. And the way he looked at her, she wasn't sure she'd ever felt so seen. Or so exposed.

She lifted up to chase his kiss but he pulled back.

"Charlotte," he said, his voice rough. Ragged. Then, on a whisper, "Charlie."

And she squeezed her eyes shut tight. And let her head drop to the bed.

He lifted over her then, the muscles in his arms

bunching beneath his shirt, then he nudged the tip of his nose against hers. She nudged back, all but purring as their faces bussed one another, in dreamy gentle strokes.

He took off his glasses, and placed them on the small table beside the bed. His lashes were imposingly long and beautifully tangled, his eyes the colour of a drift of autumn leaves.

"Were you always this gorgeous?" she asked.

He smiled at her, said, "Nah," then began to move down the bed.

He rained kisses over her jaw, down her neck, across her décolletage, before swirling his broad tongue around her right nipple, then her left. Moving on before she was ready. Keeping her hovering on the edge of the best kind of agony.

When he settled in, moving a hand over one breast while feasting on the other, for long lush minutes, her hands went to his shoulders, squeezing, frantic.

When he nipped his way down her side, before scraping his teeth over her hip bone, her hands moved to his hair, gripping, tugging, directing. She felt him smile against her belly, then he slid down her neck, between her breasts, over her navel before hooking it into her G-string and not even pausing before he dragged it down, down, down.

His arm was long enough to rid her of the thing, without having to move from where he was, his breath washing over her centre, a warm rush that had her trembling, writhing, wanting his touch. His tongue. Wanting him.

In her half-conscious state, she felt him move to the end of the bed, his knees gently hitting the floor.

She looked down her body, to find his gaze taking her in, a mix of wonder and hunger on his face, before his eyes lifted to hers. Dark as midnight and glinting with desire. Keeping her gaze, he lowered his mouth and breathed against her, a cool stream of air, before laying the gentlest of kisses at her centre.

She sobbed. Then bit her lip against her sound.

Then he slid his hands beneath her backside, and lifted her to his mouth and for the next several minutes, or eternities, she could not have said which, Beau Griffin marked his place and then some.

Sunlight glowed a weak watery gold, as it rose outside their train window. The sound of the carriage, a gently *clackety-clack*, matched the subtle sway of the bed.

Charlie, her head on Beau's chest, her thoughts running a mile a minute, tried to match his sleeping breaths, but they were too deep, too strong, and she had to suck in a deep breath so as not to faint.

"What is in your hair?" he asked, his voice rumbling beneath her cheek.

She lifted her head, her breath catching at the

sight of him—dark hair rumpled, stubble a dark shade across his jaw. "Did I wake you?"

She'd been awake for some time. Partly because she knew she'd have to be up soonish, to get ready for the post-wedding breakfast. And partly because her mind was a tumble.

For she'd slept with Beau Griffin. Knowing how important it was to get through the next few weeks with zero drama. Though the sleeping part had been the least of it. And the non-sleeping parts might well add up to the very best, most glorious, night of her entire life.

When Beau ran a hand over her hair again, then looked at his hand, she said, "Gel, hairspray, glitter. I would have washed it last night but my roommate had other plans."

His gaze moved from his hand to her face. And he breathed out and said, "Hey."

"Hey."

"Sleep okay?"

"Hardly at all."

Laughing gently, he stretched, his chest lifting her, the muscles in his arms bunching in a way that had saliva pooling beneath her tongue.

And despite her jokey tone, she felt a wave of fragility wash over her. For Beau Griffin in the morning, glasses free, after only a few hours' sleep, looked the way a guy in an ad for some expensive hotel might look. Whereas, by the way his gaze kept going back to her hair, she must have looked as if she'd slept in a cave.

She made to roll out of bed, but Beau curled his arm around her and brought her back to his chest.

"Stay," he said.

"I can't. I have to go to breakfast soon."

"Stay," he said again, and for a minute she thought he meant stay, as in don't move out of the house next door to my house so we can play neighbours, with benefits, forever.

But then his hand dropped to her back, his broad palm running down her spine, shifting the sheet that had pooled over her backside, so he could trace a finger over the curve of her cheeks. She blushed, knowing *stay* meant go another round.

"Is this really okay?" she asked.

He lifted his eyebrows.

"Us. Here. This."

He seemed to truly consider her question for a moment, which had always been one of her favourite things about him, before saying, "I reckon it's better than okay."

"Okay, good, I was just checking." Then, for good measure, because she'd never been able to hold her tongue, she added, "We don't have to put a label on what happened. We can chalk it up to circumstance. All that romance in the air. One bed. It was bound to rub off."

Beau stopped caressing her and instead put his

arm behind his head. Then he lifted his spare hand and crooked a finger.

Charlie, heart racing now, crawled a little higher up his body, the light smattering of dark hair covering the hard planes of his chest scraping against her over-sensitised skin. Once her face was level with his, he took her chin between his fingers and looked deep into her eyes.

"You know I had a crush on you, right? In senior."

Her eyes bugged. She felt it happen. "You did not."

"That final year of school, watching you make new friends, thinking constantly about that damn game of spin the bottle, kicking myself for not picking it up and placing it down so it faced only you—I was the poster boy for teen torture."

Charlie blinked at him, for none of that tracked with her experience. For one thing, she'd been the one with the crush. She'd thought he must have picked up on it, too, and that was the reason why he'd pulled away. He was too kind to tell her it was one-sided. And then...

"What game of spin the bottle?"

Beau gave her a look. "Are you kidding me right now?"

She shook her head, wracking her brain, but nothing came.

It had been a rough summer. Things with her dad had been escalating, taking on the job at the record store a final straw in his eyes. Empirical evidence that she'd amount to nothing. She'd cut her hair, pierced her nose, started wearing eyeliner and torn tights to school. And begun drinking.

When the drinking had led to true forgetting, not just the dyslexic kind, she'd given it up. Had this game happened during that time?

She shook her head, realising she was focused on the wrong thing.

Beau had *had a crush on her*. He'd told her so in a way that intimated that this wasn't just some hook up for him. But it had to be a hook up. It couldn't be anything more. For that would carve focus away from all that she was trying to achieve, for herself, on her own terms.

And yet here she was, in bed with Beau. Since it would take more willpower than she had to promise herself it wouldn't happen again, she needed to set the tone. Whatever happened from here, things had to remain as they had been between them before last night.

Before the kiss under the stars.

Before she'd kissed him on the cheek, swooning like a woman to whom this was all so much more than a hook up could ever be.

Argh!

"Look," she said, curling as his fingers began their exploration again, "last night was fun. But I really do have to get up. Breakfast is in an hour. After which the bride and groom will be dropped off, while the rest of us stay on the train as it turns around and takes us back home. You're most welcome to join us. Or find a quiet spot to... FaceTime Moose. Whatever takes your fancy."

She avoided his eyes, certain he'd feel let down by her manic backtracking. While he was being brave, and sweet, and open. A big deal for a guy going through all that he was going through.

None of which changed anything for her.

She quickly slipped out from under his arm, and didn't bother to cover up as she padded across the room and ducked into the en suite, for the night before he'd seen it all. Kissed it all. Hell, the man had licked her up and down and sideways.

In the bathroom, she leaned against the door, closed her eyes for a few moments, and re-recalibrated. Wondering how many more times she'd have to do so before their job was done.

Knowing what the answer had to be—as many as it took.

CHAPTER NINE

"So, we're two weeks out from the big day." Charlie caught the eye of a passing waiter and motioned for a bottle of water and two glasses, then mouthed her thanks.

"I know!" said Anushka, bouncing on the seat in the café.

Charlie's leg was bouncing, too, as she wanted to get home and get cleaning.

After leaving Beau in their sleeper car, she'd become a woman on a mission. Her goal, to use the train ride back to tap the wedding guests for any DIY home fixer-upper tips, so that when she got home, she could hit the ground running while she was still here. Turned out cleaning the place out before stripping the wallpaper got the most votes.

Her new goal was to spend every spare minute doing just that. Then, when she was ready to leave, she could do so knowing she'd left the house in a better place than how she'd found it.

If it meant avoiding Beau all day, avoiding what

would no doubt be a look of disappointment on his face that she wanted to keep things cool, win-win.

The drive home from the station in his sexy rocket car had been quiet. As if once they'd stated their positions, neither had more to say on the issue.

When he'd pulled up outside her front veranda, angling the car light so she could see her way safely to the door, she'd held her overnight bag to her chest, readied herself to uncurl herself from the car, thank him for his help, then bolt inside.

Super mature, but effective to her cause.

Instead, when she'd alighted the car, he'd reached for her hand and swung her against the car. His hand delving gently into her hair. His jaw working, his eyes dark, and fierce. As if he'd managed to give her the space she wanted all day, but had hit his limit.

She could have slipped away, and he'd not have stopped her.

But no. Heart racing, lady parts rejoicing, ramparts crumbling at their first test, she'd dumped her bag at her feet, lifted to her toes, pulled Beau's head to hers, and kissed the man for all she was worth.

So much for keeping things cool. Her lips had been swollen, stubble rash covering her cheeks, for a good day.

"And how's it all going?" Charlie asked Anushka after gulping down her glass of water.

"Great. So, so great. I can't even with the greatness!"

Charlie cocked her head. "You do realise that I'm the one person you don't have to pretend for."

Anushka drew in a small breath, then let rip. About a swan situation. About her mother, a woman of humble means, having a breakdown at not being able to contribute. About a pimple that wouldn't go away. About Bobby's decision to change the groomsmen's outfits after seeing Beau in a suit. Anushka winced at the last. "Is that me complaining about you?"

"It's my job to fix any annoyances. Shall I have a word with Beau?" Beau. Saying his name, even *thinking* his name, had her remembering his touch, his reverence, his skill.

"Oh, no!" said Anushka. "It's the first request Bobby has made regarding the whole thing. In fact, having Beau around has him completely engaged. I think he has a little crush."

Get in line, Charlie thought.

"Can I make a suggestion, regarding your mother?"

Anushka nodded. "Please."

"Let's find some way she *can* contribute. Giving a speech at the rehearsal dinner. Or ask her if she has a favourite song to play at the reception."

Anushka beamed. "Good gods you're good at this."

"That's why they pay me the big bucks."

Anushka laughed. Then slumped. "It's stressful being *the bride*," she said air quotation marks in play. "Right?"

Charlie smiled.

"Have you ever…? Or *are* you? Married? I assumed you and Beau were a thing, but… No? Yes? Wow, I can't believe I don't know this about you."

"No," Charlie assured her. Then, "Always the bridesmaid, remember?"

And while she knew that while the nature of the relationship between bride and professional bestie had a hastened sense of intimacy, and that one day she would be a mere heartbeat in Anushka's story, too, she found herself saying, "Though someone did offer once."

"Do tell!"

"Well, okay. I was living, working, overseas, and didn't know *anyone*. Then I met Richard…" She swallowed. "He was outgoing, had a lot of friends, and made it clear he adored me. He was also kind of hapless, you know? Had this—what I thought was charming—air of…needing looking after."

"Which is what you did," Anushka said, her voice gentle and kind.

"Big-time."

Standing up for those who couldn't, or just shouldn't have to, stand up for themselves was the one special skill her father had gifted her. One that made her feel good about herself, no matter what was going on in her life.

"By the time I realised how unbalanced the thing was he must have sensed my restlessness. And proposed. In the end it was that, the thought of taking care of someone who refused to do the same for me, forever, made me feel…exhausted. And sad, you know?"

"Mmm. How did he take it?"

"He traded up."

Made sure his wedding reception took place in the building in which I worked, and called me just about the worst thing you can call a woman.

Anushka sat back. "Oh, that all makes so much sense now."

"What does?"

"Well, #cakegate, of course."

Hearing that term coming from Anushka's smiling mouth, Charlie flinched so hard her brain knocked against the inside of her skull.

"Oh, gosh," said Anushka leaning forward, her expression concerned. "You've gone terribly pale. Are you okay? Oh, no, it's because I mentioned #cakegate?"

Heat crept up the back of Charlie's neck, and into her cheeks. She bit her lip in order to stop herself from asking Anushka to stop speaking.

But if Anushka knew… What was this? Some long game? A public hazing? Was she about to lose the best working opportunity she'd ever been gifted?

"I don't understand," said Charlie, in a stage whisper. "If you know about…that, then why am I here?"

Anushka had the good grace to look sheepish.

"I was hiding out in California a couple of years ago, after the whole '*Twilight* breakup' nonsense went viral. Which was absolute rubbish, by the way. I mean I looooove *Twilight*, but any man of mine can read whatever the heck floats his boat, as can I. I was there when #cakegate went down, found myself caught up in it like anyone, then realised I was feeding the machine that had stalked me."

"Then, when Martine told me all about this amazing woman who had made her wedding an absolute dream, your name rang a bell. And when I put two and two together, it felt meant to be. The two of us, rising from the ashes together."

Charlie sat forward, her forehead in her hands as she tried to recapture her breath.

"Oh, no. Oh, Charlie. I'm so sorry. I had no clue this would be such a big thing. It seemed gauche to bring it up when we didn't know one another. But now we're such friends. Aren't we?"

"Anushka, if anyone else knows—"

"They don't!" she said, crossing her heart. "At least not by my telling. I promise. Though second chances should be far easier to come by in my opinion. Falling down is easy. Picking yourself up, and dusting yourself off, and trying again, that's the real story here. But I get that it's not mine to tell."

Charlie finally looked into Anushka's sincere eyes. She *knew*. She knew about Charlie's screwup, and had hired her anyway. No, hired her *because* of it.

Charlie pushed her chair back, walked around the table, and bent down to give Anushka a huge hug.

"Friends?" Anushka asked, her voice hoarse against Charlie's ear.

"If you like it or not."

When Charlie sat back down, Anushka said, "Shall I order us each a glass of bubbly? I feel like after that we deserve one."

"Sure," said Charlie, laughing, mentally putting off painting the hall till tomorrow. "That'd be great."

Once the bubbly was ordered, Anushka sat forward. "Now, back to your Beau. He really is such a good guy. Please tell me you're not merely two beautiful old friends who sparkle every time you look at one another. Please tell me you're secretly hot and heavy."

Charlie laughed, even as images of Beau, hot and heavy, slipped into her mind again. For despite her attestation what had happened was due to one bed, and romance in the air, it simply wasn't true.

She'd wanted him. She'd craved him. Her high school crush nothing on the feelings she harboured for him now.

"And remember," Anushka said, her smile mischievous. "Now that we are such good friends, I'm the one person you don't have to pretend with."

Thankfully the bubbly arrived, giving Charlie a moment to collect herself. She lifted her glass in a toast. "To good guys."

Anushka lifted her glass. "To the women who deserve them."

Glasses clinked, the women both drank well.

Then Anushka said, "When the two of you get hitched, I will be matron of honour. It's only fair."

When Charlie choked on the bubbles, Anushka nearly fell off the chair laughing.

The next afternoon Beau met with Mike the electrician and Rob the master carpenter, who'd kindly come back to add a few extra outlets, and design the wall-to-ceiling bookshelves he'd imagined for what would now be a home office in the big back room at the house.

Leaving them to chat, he moved out onto the jutting concrete balcony, taking care, as while the "precarious lumber" had been removed, the railing was yet to be installed.

There, he glanced across to Charlie's place, hoping for another glimpse of her grappling with her back garden or tossing what looked like papers, and old clothes, into the skip that had appeared there the day after they'd returned from the train trip.

The train trip that was like a burr under his skin. A fever that would not abate. Nor would the desire to go to her, to force her to look him in the eye and tell him again it was nothing but "romance in the air" that had her letting her dress fall to the floor before crawling across that bed, to him.

Then, as if he'd willed her into view, she was there, dragging an old wooden ladder before wrangling it into place against the side of her house. She gave it a wriggle with her garden-gloved hands, then, satisfied, climbed the rickety contraption in old yellow gum boots that might as well have been clown shoes for all the grip they had.

All while wearing the hard hat he'd given her.

He laughed at the sight, while his chest felt as if it had caved in on itself, just a little, as if his heart had squeezed itself into a ball.

All of which quickly morphed into a squeeze of sudden pain when the ladder wobbled. He watched, helpless, as Charlie gripped the gutter with her forearm, one foot swinging off the ladder, before it settled again.

Then, after adjusting her hard hat, she started blithely pulling clumps of leaves from the gutter, as if nothing had happened.

It was enough to get Beau's feet moving, back inside, down the freshly sanded internal stairs, out the sliding glass doors of the granny flat, and across his yard. He was jogging by the time he reached the roses.

The urge to call her name as he closed in, to insist she get the hell down from there, built in his throat like a roar, but he knew that could be the thing that sent her tumbling. Then he whipped off his own hard hat, letting it drop to the ground, before reaching the ladder and holding on, his palms sweating, his head spinning with all the things that could have gone wrong.

Charlie, clearly feeling the sudden lack of wobbles, looked down, saw him, and smiled. Pure sunshine. It was nearly enough to clear out the chill that had settled in his bones.

Then the smile quickly turned into a frown. "What are you doing?"

"The sane thing; keeping this death trap steady so you can do whatever it is you decided had to be done."

She opened her palm, showed him the clump of dank rotting leaves she'd pulled from the gutter, then let it go, wet mush raining down on his head.

"Nice," he said. "Real mature."

"Mature is highly overrated."

Beau's chin lifted, and his eyes found hers, remembering that was a thing she used to say. Right around the time he'd started liking her in a whole new way. When the other kids at school had started pairing off, swearing, smoking, getting into trouble, and the two of them were still in their safe little bubble.

Only now, watching the pink rise in her cheeks, the way she swallowed, hard, Beau wondered if in fact he'd *not* been alone in feeling their friendship shift and change.

Then Charlie broke the spell, rolling her eyes. "Are you really going to stand there while I do this?"

"Yes, Charlie, I'm really going to stand here, and keep this ladder steady, while you clean your gutters."

Her voice was steady, and a little quiet, as she said, "You're not the boss of me."

His smile was irresistible. His own voice low as he said, "Sometimes it feels like someone should be."

Her eyes flashed. "And you think that is you? Why? Just because we slept together?"

And there it was. The real argument that had them both so heated up. Beau smiled up at her, sweet as pie, as he said, "I'd never dream as much."

She paused then, as if she'd built some narrative inside her head, and he'd gone rogue. But Beau was not having this conversation while she was half hanging off the side of a ladder that looked to be held together with trusted nails and mildew.

"As you are well aware, *Charlotte*, I have nowhere else to be. I can stand here all day. So, we can argue, or you can do what you set out to do."

Her eyes narrowed at him, before she turned back to the house and did her thing.

After a few more minutes, when she'd cleaned all she could clean without moving the ladder along, Charlie made her way down the rungs. Her backside, encased in cut-off shorts, frayed cotton dangling against her thighs, swished back and forth as she did so. Deliberately? He'd put money on it.

When she reached the bottom rung, she turned, not willing to give up the high ground. "What did you imagine was going to happen, when you came over here in such high heat?"

"Do you really want to know?" he asked, slowly releasing the ladder to find his fingers stiff.

She shook her head, as if hearing it she'd have to accept that he was out there in the world, caring about what became of her. When, from the bits she'd shared along the way, was something she'd not felt all that much.

He understood her reticence. That pressure that came from meaning something to someone, or vice versa. Add their history, how important they had been to one another's very survival once upon a time, and this tension that had been brewing between them didn't run on a singular dimension.

But neither did it have to be as complicated as she seemed determined to make it.

"We had sex."

Charlie blinked, her mouth dropping open ever so slightly, making it appear entirely kissable.

"Not just sex," he added, his voice rough. "Great sex. And I believe I made it clear that if you were amenable, I'd be open to having more great sex with you in the future."

Her throat worked, the pink blotching her cheeks had little to do with exertion. And she said, "You're not meant to talk that way."

"Says who?" he asked, laughter taking the edge off the tension riding him even now.

Her arms flung out to the sides. "I don't know. Past me?"

"I think it's time we put past Charlotte and past Beau firmly where they belong."

"In the past," she said on a sigh.

"As for present Beau and Charlie. Can we agree that what happened had nothing to do with *romance in the air* and everything to do with the fact that I am 'bonkers level' attracted to you. And if the way things unfolded is any evidence, you feel the same way about me."

Far too many emotions than he could count raced over her face—but he did catch stubbornness, desire, relief, and apprehension.

Then she lifted a finger, pointed it at him, and said, "So long as you can assure me you're not imagining anything that might go beyond the next few weeks. Because I am leaving. As soon as the house is tidied up, and my finances are squared away. I don't have the bandwidth to take on something that might…turn messy when it's all said and done."

Beau shook his head, even while he knew that for him it was too late to think in such terms. For Charlie had a habit of sweeping him into the whirlwind of her life and when she let go, the landing was never much fun.

It would hurt when they parted. Just as it had hurt when they'd parted last time. But he'd survive it. He always did.

"Would you like to hear what I'm imagining?"

She lifted a shoulder. "Why not?"

He moved in again, this time bracing his hands on either side of her shoulders. "I'm imagining kissing you, as often, and in as many places, as you will allow. But for that to happen, I need a little reassurance that you won't put yourself in danger, unnecessarily. Because nothing messes with my libido more than imagining you breaking your sweet neck."

Something he'd found himself doing since they'd come back home. Any time he heard a crash next door, or heard her car engine roar before she shot off down the road. The thought of her, hurt, caught like a burr in his fur. Not painful as such, but there, tugging when he moved wrong.

Charlie's eyes widened, then softened, as it occurred to her why his head was so ready to go there. Milly's spectre seemed to hover between them a moment before fading away.

"I'm wearing your hard hat," she said.

Beau lifted a hand and moved it so it sat a little farther back on her head. "If a bird flies over and drops something on it, then you'll be glad you did."

She looked down at her hands in their over-sized gloves, then at her gum boots too big for her feet, the splintered ladder rung on which she stood. And her shoulders slumped.

Then she lifted her eyes to his and said, "Anushka knows. About #cakegate. She's okay with it, she says, and that she'd not told anyone. And yet…"

Beau let out a hard breath, as the implications sank in. "That's why you needed to clean your own gutters using a rusty ladder."

"Seemed as good a way to shake off the terror that I'm this close to getting what I want and it still all might be taken away."

He reached for her and she leaned in, wrapping her arms about his neck. He lifted her off the ladder and carried her to safety before he set her down. She looked up at him, this wild, beautiful, stubborn, mess of a human.

While he knew his level of concern was excessive, to him it was a real thing. And while she wasn't exactly cliff diving, or playing Russian roulette, her presence made him feel a level of low-key tumult he could not deny.

Now, when he was finally coming out the other end of months of such inner turmoil. Now, when he was sure he never wanted to feel that way again.

"Beau?"

Beau glanced over his shoulder to see the back of Mike's hard hat on the other side of the roses.

"Coming," he called. Then, to Charlie, "I have to go. Can I see you soon? Or do you have to re-plumb the house?"

"I do not."

"No? No roofing that you're desperate to get on top of?"

"Not today," she said with a sweet smile. "I will finish the gutter, and I will take care doing so. And when I'm done, I'm going to have a long hot shower, and wash off this grime." Then, "Care to join me?"

With a growl in his throat, one for himself as much as for her, Beau leaned down, bending Charlie back so that she had to hold on tight. Then he kissed her throat, the bare skin just below, before lifting her up just enough to find her mouth.

All of it, any lingering concern, the fact that she was fixing to leave, right when he was putting in measures that gave him an option to stay, dissolved in the heat of that kiss.

When he pushed his way back through the rose bushes a minute later, he looked back to see her lining up the ladder, this time her bare feet gripped the ladder, the gardening gloves were tucked into the back of her shorts till she had purchase.

The peach-coloured hard hat remained.

Beau, watching the leaves rustle in the forest in the valley beyond, looked up when Charlie's back door squeaked.

She stood on the landing and stretched her arms overhead. Then she slipped her shirt over her head, dropped it at her feet and went inside. A second later her back light switched on.

Beau laughed out loud.

Then called, "Nearly done?" to Mike, who was finishing packing up.

"Yep. Anything else you need, or if Moose needs a babysitter, give me a buzz."

Beau shook his hand, then ushered the man out the front door as fast as was humanly possible.

A minute later, as he jogged up Charlie's the back steps, he looked to that weak single light, doing little to light up her big open backyard.

He brought out his phone, and sent Mike a quick message. All the while knowing he wasn't about to win any favours. But if it meant he slept better that night, and all the nights after, he was willing to take the hit.

He picked up the shirt Charlie had dropped, and followed the trail—bra, shorts, gardening gloves—then followed the sounds of running water till he found what must have been Charlie's bedroom. Faded green quilt with pink stitching crumpled on the bed, a pair of mismatched pillows. Clothes draped over a single lounge seat in one corner.

Steam pouring from an open en suite door.

Then a hand appeared, holding the peach hard hat, before she tossed it to the bed, her hand trailing becomingly back into the bathroom.

Beau stripped faster than any man in the history of stripping, and strutted into the bathroom so fast she screamed. Then laughed, raucously, as he hauled her into the shower.

And there the laughter stopped. Making way for sighs, and gasps. The slide of slippery hands and slow wet kisses. Losing themselves in one another. Till the water turned cold.

After drying off, they'd wrapped themselves in blankets and padded out to the kitchen to eat the best leftover pasta of Beau's life. Then dug into a chocolate torte she'd whipped up that morning, devouring it with a pair of mismatched spoons, while telling stories of heartbreaks and bad dates, embarrassing gaffes and moments that made them feel proud.

Then she walked him to the front door, hand

in hand, before he'd turned her to the wall, one hand braced beside her head, his thumb stroking her neck as he kissed her. His other hand peeling the blanket apart, leaving just enough room to slide his hand between her legs. The sweep of his tongue in her mouth mirroring the slide of his fingers, till she gasped against his kiss, and shuddered under his touch.

With one last kiss to her forehead, he left, heading back to his rental and his goofball of a dog.

Wondering how the hell he was going to get over her a second time.

CHAPTER TEN

"IS THIS NECESSARY?" Beau asked, more to himself than the dance studio at large.

"Mate," said Bobby, bouncing from foot to foot, rolling out his neck, as if he was about to engage in a little light cage fighting rather than a dance lesson. "If I have to be here, then as my best man, so do you. That's the deal."

Beau was fairly sure the deal had more to do with being on the outer with Charlie, yet again.

For when, the night after their "shower," she'd discovered Beau had had Mike fix her back porch lights, the things now illuminating her backyard so it looked like daylight, she'd called, and not to say thank you.

"Seriously?" she'd said by way of hello.

Beau, who was taking a dog behaviour lesson he'd organised through the local vet, said, "I think the term you're looking for is thank you."

He mouthed sorry to the instructor, who rolled her eyes as if it was clear why Moose was unmanageable.

"For what?" she shot back. "Thinking me incapable?"

"Of being an electrician without a license, hell yes."

A pause, but only so she could rev herself up again. "Did you not hear me tell you that the men I've known haven't been all that interested in my advice, or opinions. Or…what was the other…skill sets!"

"I am interested in all those parts of you, as well as many other parts. I can even name them if you'd like. Starting with the freckle next to your left—"

"Beau," Charlie had growled.

While the dog behaviour instructor's eyes went a little wide at that one.

Beau took a few long strides away. "Charlie, I know that you are highly capable. I also know you well enough to know that despite your opinion being wrong on this one, you were stubborn enough to try."

And the thought of that happening, when he wasn't there…

Another long beat slunk by before she said, "I just… I spent the past year and a half hearing my father's voice following me through the house, telling me I was kidding myself thinking I could start again. Then, a while ago, it stopped and I'd gotten used to imagining doing all these things to the house, even though I'll likely get around to like three percent of them."

Beau held a hand to his forehead. "I understand. I won't do it again. But I can't promise not to come at you with slides, and graphs, and pie charts if I know I'm right."

At that she'd laughed, before ringing off, and his relief had been immense.

That had been three days ago. And what with work pouring into his inbox, work he was finding himself looking forward to again, time felt as if it was speeding up with the wedding ten days away, and his house all but done.

"Clap-clap," called the instructor, clapping her hands at the same time. Dust motes swirled in the streams of sunlight pouring through the old arched windows of the dance studio.

Then she looked to the two men—Beau, at six foot four, towering over both her and Bobby—and narrowed her eyes, as if she was up for the challenge.

Bobby leaned toward Beau. "You thinking what I'm thinking?"

"That she's wondering if I can lift you over my head?"

"Exactly."

Then—

"Sorry we're late!"

Beau and Bobby breathed out in unified relief, and turned as Anushka burst into the studio wearing a bright pink leotard, fluorescent yellow tights and blue leg warmers. She dumped a huge tie-dyed duffel bag on a bench by the door, jogged over to Bobby, and leaped into his arms for a kiss.

That all happened out of the corner of Beau's eye as his gaze remained trained on the bench, where Charlie sat, shucking off her shoes and frowning at her phone.

After a few moments she placed the phone face down, took a moment to collect herself, then pressed herself from the bench and walked their way.

Beau could hear Anushka chattering about how they'd gotten lost, then stopped for a drive-through milkshake because she was so dehydrated, but it was all background noise.

For all he could see was Charlie. Her hair pulled back in a loose bun. A cropped black tank top, a long black skirt that sat low on her hips and swished around her ankles as she walked. She looked beautiful, and fragile. And tired.

He swallowed against a lump in his throat as it occurred to him that even if he was able to hold her ladder for her now, fix all her broken light-bulbs, there would always be more. And he'd not be around to see them.

"Hey, stranger," he said as she walked up beside him, avoiding his eyes.

"Enough chatter!" the instructor called.

Anushka jumped, leaping into the space beside

Bobby, who grabbed her hand, kissed it, tucked it into the crook of his arm. While Beau and Charlie might as well have been on opposite sides of the room.

The instructor, Mariana, positioned the couples into a correct dance hold. Lifting hands and placing them where they ought to go. Squaring shoulders, tipping chins high. Moving feet into position with a sharp kick of a dance shoe against the instep.

She hummed happily at Anushka and Bobby, then tsked at Charlie and Beau, before pushing their torsos closer together.

"Music!" said Mariana, before she tapped over to an ancient boom box and a song broke out. Some sultry French number, all snare drums and hazy trumpets. "Now we dance!"

"What do you reckon?" Beau crooned as he pulled Charlie a smidge closer. "Do we go with the 'Macarena'?"

Bobby snickered, and Anushka shushed him. While Charlie's gaze finally flickered to Beau.

"Oh, hi, look who showed up."

She narrowed her eyes at him, then looked away. Beau pressed a gentle finger under her chin and moved her head back to face him. When her eyes found his again, he nodded. *There*.

"Move. Feet. Glide!" Mariana called.

Eyes on one another, Beau swayed with the

music, unsurprised to find Charlie fought him the whole way.

"Why exactly are we here?" he asked, when no more instructions came their way.

"Moral support?" Charlie said.

Beau looked to Anushka and Bobby who were watching them with big smiles on their faces, before quickly looking away.

"They're matchmaking," Charlie chided.

"It would seem so. Should we tell them we're doing okay without them? For proof, I can tell them about the freckle on your left—"

Charlie smacked him on the chest, then left her hand there.

Beau took his chance to pull her closer. "Is it the light thing?"

"Is what the light thing?"

"The fact I've not seen you in three days."

"I've been busy."

Beau swung her in a circle. Whooping, in surprise, she gripped his shoulders, before looking to him with wide eyes when he went back to swaying.

When he said nothing else, she filled the silence with, "It's kind of the light thing. But not in the way you think."

Beau swept them a little farther away from the wedding couple, who were showing Mariana a move they wanted to incorporate into their wedding dance routine. And again, left silence for Charlie to fill.

"I was upset. But I also knew your intention was never to best me, the way my dad always had. Meaning my righteous indignation lasted about thirty seconds before I saw your actual intention. Which was looking out for me."

She looked to him then, her soft mossy green eyes bright with vulnerability, as she said, "Yes?"

"Yes."

She blinked several times in quick succession. "I've never had anyone be that person for me before. I can't get used to it, Beau. It's just… I can't." Her intimation being that she'd miss it, miss him, when this was all said and done. "But you won't stop, will you?"

"Won't stop, can't stop," he admitted.

And she gave him a look that seemed to say, *Watch out, Beau Griffin, you know not what you want.* And while he'd thought exactly the same thing not all that long ago, now he wasn't so sure.

"It seems we are at an impasse," said Beau as he pulled her against him. With a sigh she leaned her head against his chest. He wondered if she could feel it, the thunder and lightning crashing inside him.

In the recent past that level of feeling usually heralded a bout of high anxiety, but this felt less like existential dread, and more like…life. The flint of snapping nerves, the chemistry of warming skin. Part and parcel of being around Charlie.

The music stopped, mid-song. Beau felt Charlie flinch against him. He took his time slowing the sway, wanting this moment, her body molten against his, to a last a little longer. Forever if possible.

"That was brilliant!" Anushka called out from the other end of the room. "Did you guys work out any moves? We came up with a couple of bangers. We may yet look like newborn giraffes, but it'll be a blast."

Mariana looked unimpressed, as she stood by her boom box, wiping down her hands with a wet wipe.

"We have to go," said Anushka. "Couples massage time. Wanna join?"

Charlie looked to Beau, and lifted an insouciant shoulder. *Yes?* she mouthed.

Beau, eyes wide, shook his head infinitesimally. *Noooooo.*

Charlie laughed, then quickly wiped a finger under one eye, as she said, "Not for us."

"Okay. See you later!" Anushka tucked her arm into Bobby's, and they were gone.

Beau and Charlie made their way over to the bench where Charlie shucked her thongs back onto her feet.

"What next?" Beau asked.

And Charlie looked into his eyes. It was a big question. Go forward, step backward, either way knowing there was an end point coming.

"Coffee?" she asked, deliberately misunderstanding.

Which was fine with him.

He reached out an arm, offering refuge, and with a small smile, she stepped in. He wrapped her tight, laying a kiss to the top of her head. The scent of her—warm, delicate, a hint of heat—was like a balm. It soothed weary limbs. Mended broken hearts. Lit up broken souls.

He also felt the end rushing at him now. Only this time, since he saw it coming, he could prepare. Well in advance.

"Time to go!" Mariana called, and they both flinched. "Next students due soon."

"Yep!" said Charlie, putting her arms around his waist, and tucked in tight to one another, as both were soaking up every moment they had left, they ambled out of the dance studio together.

It was the week before the wedding and with Beau on-site keeping the builders honest, his house had come together more quickly than expected. It was, for all intents and purposes, habitable.

Which was great, as Charlie could stickybeak without need for gum boots or hard hat. Though considering the things she'd done with Beau while wearing that hat, it would have a very special place in her heart forever more.

Then, right as she started thinking that maybe, just maybe, it would all go as smoothly as could be, Beau announced Matt and his kids—Milly's kids—were coming to visit.

Anushka, having found out about the completed house, and Beau's friend's imminent arrival, had insisted they have their final wedding war meeting double up as a housewarming, and convinced Beau to give her a budget to "spiff the place up."

Which she did. With panache. In three days the place was decked out with art on the walls, the kitchens and bathrooms fully fitted out, lux couches and solid tables, and beautiful natural decor in every room, until it was as far from a weapons facility as a space could be.

While Beau drove to the airport to pick up the guests of honour who, he assured her, *were excited to see for themselves what I love about the place*, Charlie sat on his balcony, spiralling. Even more than she had with "the light" thing. Or the "sleeping together" thing.

For while she might be dyslexic as heck, she could read between the lines just fine. If Matt was as smart as a business partner of Beau's must be, he was coming to bring his boy back home.

It was laughable really. There she'd been, imagining the day she had the house ready, money in the bank, standing by her front gate, a hand to Beau's stricken face as she told him it had been lovely, before she hopped into a taxi and was swept away.

Romantic—and karmic—as she made it sound, she wasn't delusional. They had become so close, so fast, she was so used to having him near, that it would be fraught as all hell. She may have retired to the shower to ugly cry over it more than once.

But what had *not* occurred to her—as Beau had forged a connection to his new house, the town, the locals who had fallen for him here—was that he might be the one to leave her. Again.

While Beau drove to the Sunshine Coast Airport, to pick up the guests of honour, Charlie curled up in a big outdoor chair on his upstairs deck, making her way through her second glass of bubbly. While Phyllida and Jazmin, Anushka's bridesmaids, ran about in circles, stressing and generally getting in the way, Anushka was a seasoned general, ordering Bobby's groomsmen to hang the chunky outdoor string lights just so.

And then there were voices from front of the house.

Beau was back.

Charlie quickly uncurled herself from her chair, and stood, not quite sure where to put her hands. For they were shaking; nerves, panic that she might do something, say something, that would force events that hurt her in the end. It wouldn't be the first time.

Then Beau was there, accepting cheek kisses and shaking hands, as he led his friend through his beautiful home, with its wide hall, high ceilings, and bright clean lines, its warm wood and vintage accents. A wave of feeling came over her—a mix of nostalgia with some glimpse of the future, as if she was watching him through a time slip.

With every step, she waited for him to look up. Readying herself for the catch of his eyes, warm and bright behind his glasses, the half smile that would tug at his mouth, the certainty that he was happy she was there.

Then a pair of small humans bolted past him— one with curly blond hair flying out behind her, the other dragging a blanket nearly as big as himself.

"Uncle Bobo!" said the girl. *Tasha*, Charlie reminded herself. "Where's Moose?"

"Wherth Moothe?" lisped the boy. *Drew*. Who, blanket in hand, thumb wedged in his mouth, reached back to take Beau's hand.

Beau, who was listening to Bobby tell a story about some statue he'd stopped Anushka from buying on his behalf, slowly crouched down, so as to give his attention to both.

A fist closed around Charlie's heart. It was so swift, and so punishing, she had to brace herself so as not to crumple.

That was when Beau's gaze found hers. He lifted his spare hand in a simple wave and smiled. A smile of joy at seeing her. And something else. Understanding as to why she was outside, on her own.

Before she gave herself away completely, Charlie made to head inside, when Beau stood and called Matt's name. And the illusive Matt, business partner and best friend, the one whose marriage, whose wife, had sent Beau down this path of self-reflection, came through the kitchen door.

A smidge shorter than Beau, he was dressed down in a Henley T-shirt, scarf, and khakis. The guy was easy on the eyes, and widowed some eight months. Charlie was suddenly afraid Jazmin and Phyllida might attempt to eat him alive.

Beau said something to him, while twisting Drew and now Tasha around in circles at the ends of his hands, and Matt glanced outside. Pinning her with a focused gaze.

Gripping her now-empty glass of bubbly, she had second thoughts about the floral strapless dress she wore. Wish she'd forgone the diamanté barrette. Or toned down the bright pink lip.

But this was a *party*. Anushka and Bobby's, as well as Beau's. So, stuff it. Stuff 'em all.

She squared her shoulders, as Beau stepped out onto the balcony, his eyes leaving hers only long enough to take in the decor, the fairy lights, how clean the place was.

"How was this even possible?" he asked.

"Anushka," said Charlie with a shrug. "Phyl and Jaz tried their best to unhinge the afternoon, while I sat back, drank bubbly, and watched. It's been a treat."

He slid his hand to her waist, pulled her close

and bussed a kiss to her cheek. Murmuring against her ear, "That's my girl. Smarter than the rest by a country mile."

His girl. *His girl.* The urge to laugh, hysterically, bubbled up in her throat. While at the same time she melted into him, because that was how she rolled.

"Now. Charlie." Charlie jumped as Beau's voice shifted into mad mode. "I'd like you to meet my business partner, Matt Van Patten. Matt, this is Charlotte Goode."

"Hey, Matt," she said, reaching out a hand. "How was the flight?"

"Did you not see the two ratbags who are my travelling companions?" Then, looking around, "Actually, have you seen my two ratbags?"

"I've got them!" a female voice called.

And Matt relaxed.

"Great. Sorry." He wiped his hands down the sides of his jeans before taking her hand. "Charlotte, hello."

"You can call me Charlie," she said.

"Charlie," he said, with a quick smile. While his eyes, sharp and bright, judged her with all the judging a sharp-minded, business-savvy, nice-looking widower in his early thirties could muster.

"Beau!" That was Anushka who was flipping his kitchen cupboards open and closed. "Cups for the kids? Do you have a preference?"

"Excuse me," said Beau, shooting Charlie an "I'll be right back" smile, then glaring at Matt before he ambled inside. He was all loose-limbed and relaxed, the king of his castle. Making her think, *Surely, he couldn't give this up?*

"So, what do you think of the house?" Charlie asked, dragging her gaze back to Matt. And if Matt noticed the effort that took, he kindly didn't show it.

He looked back inside where the small group were chatting and laughing and lounging about, then out at the view with its smattering of white clouds lit silver by the moonlight.

"It's…phenomenal."

The thread of surprise beneath the words made Charlie sure her take on his visit was correct.

"I hear he has you to thank for that," said Matt.

"Me?"

"The last-minute changes he made—such as the wood panelling out front, the polished floors, the linen wallpaper? I got the feeling this place was going to be a monument to the colour grey, till you made it clear he could do better."

Charlie's gaze snapped to Beau, who was leaning against the kitchen bench, making Tasha laugh as he drank something from a blue plastic cup.

Matt sighed. "Far out, it's good to see him smiling."

She looked back to Matt, to see that his own

smile didn't quite reach his eyes. No wonder—
he'd lost his wife, and his best friend had moved
away, within months of one another.

Charlie found herself saying, "He's really
happy you guys are here."

"Yeah?" Matt laughed, the sound soft. As if he
hadn't been sure. As if he was on the fence as to
what *his* next move should be.

And she realised then that Matt was no bogey-
man, out to upend her life. They were, all of them,
trying to get by as best they could.

"He talks about you all the time. He adores
your kids. Jury is out on the dog."

Matt laughed softly. "Yeah. Big energy that
one."

"It's clear Beau was awfully fond of Milly, too."

Matt blinked, his face crumpling, and Charlie stilled.

"Oh, my God, I'm so sorry. Was that the wrong
thing—?"

"No," said Matt, putting a hand on her wrist,
then curling it back away when he remembered
they'd just met. "Most people are so careful
around me, they never bring her up in case it up-
sets me. As if I'm not thinking about her every
moment of every day."

She honestly couldn't imagine. "What was she
like? If it's okay to ask."

"Sure. Sure. She was crazy smart. Pretty, too.
No bullshit. Way out of my league." When Matt

looked in her direction again, his expression had changed. As if he truly saw her for the first time. He leaned against the balustrade and said, "Beau's really talked about her?"

Charlie nodded. "He said you guys took him under your wings when you first met. I get the feeling she made it her mission to civilise him. At first, I wasn't sure I liked the sound of that."

Matt lifted a brow.

Charlie looked to Beau in the kitchen and said, "I'd spent so many years trying to un-civilise him, to rumple him, get him to lose the pocket calculator and play hooky every now and then. I worried she'd undone all my good work."

At that Matt truly laughed. His head falling back as the sound spilled out into the night.

Beau, hearing it, turned shocked eyes their way. And mouthed, *He okay?*

She gave him a quick thumbs-up.

When he lifted a hand to his chest, in thanks, she knew—her feelings for this man were gargantuan. Great gusty clouds of warmth and adoration and lust. If he left first, or she did, it was going to break her heart in two.

"So that's how it is," Matt said.

And Charlie glanced over to find his gaze moving between her and Beau, his brow furrowed in a way that made her heart hurt for him.

"What? No. I mean… No." Yes. *Big-time yes.*

But not for much longer, so not for him to worry about.

"Right. Okay. Sorry. Beau did mention that you're looking to head off pretty soon. Off on some grand adventure?"

"Um…yes. Well, my mum is travelling the wilds of Scotland these days. And I haven't seen her for a while. So, I'm thinking a move to Edinburgh might be just the ticket."

It was the first time she'd said it out loud, and her heart lurched, with equal parts anticipation and panic.

"Your work can transfer there easily enough?" Matt asked.

"People fall in love and get married the world over, so sure. All I'll need is a couple of gigs, to show people what I do, and if it's anything like here, it will snowball pretty quickly. I've been thinking I might even keep the branch here going, as I have an offsider," aka Julia the bookkeeper, "who would be super keen to take it on."

"Love it," Matt said, then he yawned. And laughed. And held up both hands in submission. "Forgive me. I have two kids under five. This is my first grown-up night out in months. On that note I'd better go rescue whoever has them."

He reached out a hand and placed it gently on her arm. "It was really nice meeting you, Charlie. I hope the move goes brilliantly."

"It was great meeting you, too," she said, somehow keeping the smile on her face as Matt headed inside in search of Drew and Tasha.

After which Charlie collapsed back into the chair; a stream of air escaping her mouth as she let her head fall back with a clunk.

She'd been living in a dreamland this whole time. Fusing smart, sweet teenage Beau on whom she'd had a secret crush with *this* Beau. A man who, when he wasn't "taking time off," ran a multimillion-dollar business. A man who had an entire life, and people who loved him, who needed him, a thousand kilometres away.

Not that she'd had any dreams of it all working out somehow—Beau and Charlie, together forever. Except she *had* had those dreams. Years and years ago. And more recently, when she'd not been on top of her thoughts.

Maybe if he were still broken, maybe *that* Beau would be right for her. But he was doing so much better, smiling, enjoying himself, back working, even if from home, each day. And according to the person who knew him best these days, they all had her to thank for his turnaround.

She'd screwed up her chances, by *not* screwing up. It was too deliciously ironic to cope.

The next morning the kids were plonked in front of *Bluey* on a downstairs TV, Moose lying between them, loving the little hands playing with his ears. Matt and Beau sat in the shade of the balcony, looking out over the view.

Matt, groaning as the lifted his feet to the coffee table, said, "Last night was fun."

"Glad you enjoyed it."

"But Bobby Freaking Kent? You might have warned me about that? I think my tongue hit the ground before I had the chance to wind it back in."

Beau laughed, rolling a bottle of cold water over the back of his neck before taking a swig. Then found Matt watching him.

"You seem better," Matt said.

"I am. Not all the way, but getting there. On that I want to thank you, again, for letting me go."

"I pushed you as I remember it. It was what you needed. While I needed to stay. No thanks are necessary."

"I can't help feeling I left you in the lurch."

"Something Milly and I realised, right back at the beginning, that you've never quite caught on to, is that Luculent isn't a company that makes green engines, Luculent is whatever we decide it should be. And I'm not sure any of us can expect to come out of this the same as what we were."

Beau breathed out hard, understanding what Matt was telling him. That for all that he was working again, their little company was still very much in flux.

"I have something else, Luculent-related, to tell you, if you're up to hearing it."

"Something good?"

"Something very good. We've had word. The LE has progressed to final testing."

Beau sat up. "Are you kidding me?"

The majority of patents in their field fell by the wayside long before they even reached this point. Whether by way of safety concerns, sustainability, becoming redundant by the time it was their turn, or pressure from outside forces.

Matt, grinning from ear to ear, shook his head.

Beau leaned over and smacked him on the knee, before both men hugged as if they'd won the lotto.

"I can swing the reports your way—" Matt offered.

"Now. Please."

Matt pulled out his phone, fiddled some, then Beau's phone began to ping.

Meaning he was distracted when Matt said, "So, Charlie the neighbour seemed nice."

Beau let his phone drop to his lap. "That she is."

"You know what I liked even better—how you were when she was around."

Beau picked up the bottle of water, then put it back on the table. "Did she say anything to you about…"

"Edinburgh. Visiting her mum. Starting over." Matt leaned forward. "I tell you this because while I understand that we are feeling our way here, I am a selfish human person who wants you to come home."

Beau looked around at the two-bedroom apartment he'd had fitted out underneath his house. The one he'd imagined Matt and the kids could use. While their entire operation went on without them a thousand kilometres away?

"Yeah," Beau said, frowning at his hands.

"But I guess that all depends," said Matt. "If *you* like who you are when she's around."

Beau ran his hand over his jaw. "Charlie isn't like other people. She's fierce, and protective, and unexpected. But she's also extremely fragile. I'm not sure if I trust that she can do this."

"And yet?"

Beau looked to the man who'd become more than a friend. "I also think she's inevitable."

"Man," said Matt laughing softly, clearly loving seeing Beau on his metaphorical knees. "Been there."

"Worth it?" Beau asked, already knowing Matt's answer.

"Every damn time."

The men sat in silence for a moment before:

"Dad! Dad! Dad!" the kids called in tandem.

Matt looked over and raised a hand to let them know he was coming, before laying it on Beau's back. "It must be the 'Sleepytime' episode. I cry every time and the kids think it's hilarious."

Beau raised his water bottle in salute as Matt went to be with his kids.

Then after a few long beats, he pictured himself walking into the house as he had the night before, only to find it empty, Charlie on the opposite side of the world.

After which he pressed himself to standing before heading inside to watch the kids watch what was his favourite *Bluey* episode, too.

He'd get to the life stuff later.

In the week leading up to Anushka's wedding, Charlie helped a bride write vows in which every line referred to a Harry Styles lyric; took another to a favourite vintage store to pick out an inexpensive diamanté tiara; and spent four hours sitting at the hairdressers making sure yet another bride's hair turned out the exact same shade of honey blond as Rachel in season two of *Friends*.

But she was winding down, having not taken on any new "wedding day" clients after she'd booked Anushka. Meaning when her current list was done, she had nothing to keep her fettered here.

Which of course always brought her back to Beau.

She'd only seen him in passing, since the housewarming. He was busy taking Matt and the kids to the beach, to Australia Zoo, to Montville. Still trying to convince them to "love the place like he did" or his way of saying goodbye?

Then, as rain had started pattering against her bedroom window the night before the wedding, her phone rang.

"Beau?" she said in lieu of hello.

"Do you always answer the phone that way?" he asked, his voice deep, and tired, and her favourite sound in the whole world.

"Always," she said, muting *My Best Friend's Wedding* on the TV on her dresser, and snuggling back into her bed. She held a pillow to her chest in lieu of the thing she wished was really there. "You sound rough."

"I feel rough. I thought Moose was a handful but Tasha and Drew and Moose together are a tornado."

"I bet. Do you think that means they're ready to take the big guy back?"

A pause, then, "We've decided he's staying with me."

"Did *we* now?" she said, imagining Beau putting up an argument as to why that should be. The warmth in her chest bloomed all the more.

"Are you ready for tomorrow?" she asked. "Any last-minute best man nerves? Or questions about what you have to do?"

"Not a one. I'll just follow your lead."

Charlie looked to the ceiling, silently shouting at the gods as to why they'd not made more like this one.

"So," she said, "I guess this isn't a booty call,

then. Pity, because I'm here in my sexiest night attire."

"I did just drop Matt and the kids at the airport."

"Oh. Then would you like to come over?"

Charlie heard a knock at the door.

She looked up, then at her phone, then dumped it on the bed as she bolted for the front door. She whipped it open to find Beau standing there, his phone to his ear.

His hair was damp. The shoulders of his T-shirt covered in wet splotches. He looked like a man who'd spent a week with two young kids and a harried single dad. He also looked like he was ready to eat her up on the spot.

The thought of not having him in her life anymore hurt so much she moaned.

He put his phone in his back pocket, his voracious gaze raking her up and down.

"Sexiest night attire?" he queried.

She glanced down at her track pants and faded Dsylexia Sukcs T-shirt. Before whipping the shirt over her head.

After a beat Beau was over the threshold and in her arms, kissing her neck, her cheeks, her lips as he lifted her off her feet and pressed her against the hallway wall.

"The front door," she managed.

He reached back with a long leg and kicked it shut.

"I've missed the hell out of this," he said, pressing his mouth to hers. "I've missed you."

His hands moved to her backside, pulling her against his hard ridge.

"Serves you right for having other friends," she said.

"Mmm," he said, now only half listening as he pulled back to run his hands over her shoulders, his thumbs dipping into her clavicles, then he slid an arm behind her back arching her to his mouth.

Charlie's eyes slammed shut as sensation rocked through her. Feeling, and heat, and the knowledge that she missed him, too. Already. Even now.

"Beau," she said, as the rain began to pour down outside, her hands tugging on his damp hair.

"Charlie," he breathed back, his voice ragged with emotion.

Then not another word was said for a long time.

CHAPTER ELEVEN

THE STORM BROKE early the next morning, leaving Anushka and Bobby's wedding day perfect, crisp, and bright. And while Charlie knew that controlling the weather was outside her purview, since the moment she'd woken up, she'd been quietly freaking out.

"It's all going to be fine," she said out loud to the mirror in the powder room of the Kents' fabulous hinterland estate. "It's all going to be fine."

All the while her internal monologue chanted, *Don't screw up, don't screw up, don't screw up.*

It had nothing to do with the size of the place, the mixing of cultures and families and money and celebrity, the security at the head of the driveway and paparazzi helicopters already flying overhead. For her job was as it ever was—keep the bride happy while fending off any slings and arrows coming her way.

It was the amount riding on the day, *personally*, that had her stomach in knots.

After today she'd have enough money in the bank to have real choices.

After today she and Beau had no reason to see one another, except to see one another.

After today her sole focus *had* to be what came next.

Giggling in the hall outside the powder room drew her attention, before the door swung open and Anushka's bridesmaids, Phyllida and Jazmin, spilled in.

"Hey," said Charlie. "Why aren't you with Anushka?"

One hiccupped, while the other giggled uncontrollably. Brilliant. They were already tipsy.

"And we're off," Charlie muttered, giving her expression a good hard nod. Selfishly glad to have something else to focus on other than the roiling thoughts in her own head.

She ran a hand over her hair, stuck a hand inside the low-cut neck of her black leather dress to plump the girls, then checked her teeth for stray lipstick.

Ready, she grabbed her bag, rifling through the thing till she came up with a pill box. "Take one of these each. It's B1, which will settle your stomachs. Any allergies? No? Have some paracetamol and a huge drink of water. Then meet me in the vestibule in five minutes. If I find out Anushka

has a single clue that you are not on song, I will…
unfollow your Instagram."

Phyllida gasped, while Jazmin covered her
mouth, panic in her eyes.

Done with them, Charlie went to find her girl.
A text came through. She checked in case it was
Anushka.

It was from Beau. Whom she'd last seen when
he'd kissed her cheek before slipping back to his
own place in the middle of the night.

In case it hadn't occurred to you yet today, you
are a phenomenon. Anushka made the right decision, including you. If you're looking for me, I'll be
the one standing next to the bride…no, groom.

Charlie laughed. Read the thing again, in case
she'd misread it. Then again. Needing to wipe a
quick tear from beneath her eye.

She went to type back, but her hand was shaking. Add dyslexic spelling and it was best not.
Probably a good thing, as her gut instinct was
to write a string of superlatives, outlining all the
ways she thought him wonderful, too.

Which, at this point in the game, would be nothing short of dumb. The worst kind of self-sabotage.
For today was the tipping point between her future
and her past—the mistakes, the failures, the big
swings, the bigger misses. Get through this, and
they would soon be all behind her.

Feeling a twinge of guilt, she slipped her phone into her bag and strode toward the vestibule where Anushka awaited her.

Apart from the slight dampness on the ground, a missing uncle—found—and a trip hazard in the aisle—fixed—Anushka and Bobby's wedding went off without a hitch.

The vows were adorable, the crowd rowdy and engaged, the bride and groom themselves in every way. Anushka in her sparkly mini dress and hair in Princess Leia buns wrapped in daisies looked like a pixie princess while Bobby in his midnight black velvet suit, and well concealed lifts, was a revelation.

For Charlie, the hardest part was standing on the raised dais with Beau just across the way. He looked utterly devastating in his morning suit, like something out of a fairy tale. Making it impossible not to remember how it felt to have his mouth on her neck, his voice against her ear, his hand holding her cheek as if she was the most precious thing he'd ever known.

Making it impossible for her to do her job.

In a desperate effort to keep herself together, she made a subtle motion for him to fix his perfect boutonniere.

The grin she got in return made it all too clear he wasn't to be tricked. He knew why her eyes were on him. He knew how to make her smile, how to make warmth bloom brightly inside her, how to make her feel as if she could do and be anything.

The problem was for her to do the thing she wanted most, to curate a life of her own, one she was proud of, one she built on her own terms and no one else's, Beau couldn't be there.

Things moved quickly after that.

"Another One Bites the Dust" blared as Anushka and Bobby danced back down the aisle, while Charlie collected the fallen petals from Anushka's bouquet as the bride wanted to craft something from them later on.

During the family photographs Charlie reminded the photographer whom Bobby's mother had chosen, that there were to be some fun ones after the stuffy classics.

Once inside the ballroom for the reception, Charlie made sure to spend time with Anushka's mother, and to tell her how much she loved the poem she'd read during the sermon.

Then came time for the first dance. As promised—and witnessed firsthand during that final dance lesson—Anushka and Bobby were a joyful mess. The routine was a little waltz, a little hustle, a little interpretive movement ballet, with Anushka and Bobby tripping over one another, and not even close to being on time with the beat.

Then Anushka's gaze found Charlie's in the

crowd. She clicked her hand at Charlie, mouthing, *Save us!*

Before Charlie even had to look for Beau he was there beside her, hand out, drawing her onto the dance floor.

Only rather than hold her the way he had in their "lesson," he lifted her till her feet rested on his, much to the delight of the crowd.

"So much for letting me lead the way," Charlie murmured, wrapping her hands around Beau's neck and holding on for dear life.

"Everywhere but here. And in the bedroom. And on a construction site."

"My options are shrinking before my eyes." She said it as a joke, but the truth of it was all too real.

As if he saw it in her eyes, some pulling back, or some pain, Beau's eyes narrowed in question.

Charlie, the coward, looked down at their feet. "Am I hurting you?"

"I own protective shoes for all occasions."

As Anushka and Bobby had separated and pulled as many others who would join them onto the dance floor, Beau's movements slowed, till *they* were swaying gently.

"Are we having fun?" Beau asked.

"My goal is for Anushka and Bobby to have fun. My enjoyment is secondary."

"What about my enjoyment?" he asked, spinning her so fast she closed her eyes and squealed.

"Eighth," she said when he slowed. "Seventh at the very most."

He leaned back so that she was looking into his eyes as he said, "I'll take it." And she believed him, too.

How little he asked of her, how solid in his own shoes.

Before she could stop herself, she tilted her head and kissed him, a soft slow caress into which she poured all the feelings surging inside her. He lifted her so that her feet were airborne, and deepened the kiss, as he was doing the same.

He slowly let her feet fall back to the floor, waited till she had purchase, then moved her around the floor with more grace, and caution, and sweetness than she thought possible.

You're okay, she thought. *He's okay. We will be okay.*

She waited for her internal monologue to perk up with some sassy comment to the contrary, but for once it stayed quiet.

When the song ended, and the crowd cheered, she forced the swaying to a stop and said, "I have to check on the cake."

The cake? Where did that come from? She did *not* have to check on the cake. She wanted nothing to do with the cake. What she needed was to breathe air that did not smell like him, so she could get her head on straight. For right now it felt anything but.

"Go get 'em," Beau said, twirling her out to the end of his arm, kissed her hand, then let her go. Then he curled a finger toward Anushka who began to draw herself to him with an invisible rope. Taking up where she left off, without having to be asked.

"You're the best, bestie!" Anushka called out.

Charlie lifted her hand in a wave as she shot off the dance floor.

"My daughter is so lucky she found you," Mrs. Patel said, hugging her as she passed.

She managed a thumbs-up.

"I'm calling you Monday," said a young woman, grabbing her by the elbow and looking intently into her eyes. "From what I hear, you are a genius," said another, "and I must have you."

She kept walking, not in the right headspace to explain that she *couldn't* take them on. That she was leaving. Unless they wanted to get married in Edinburgh? Was it Edin-burg, or Eden-bor-ough? She wasn't even sure how to pronounce it properly, but for some reason she'd decided that's where she was going to start over.

She heard Beau's voice saying, *Wherever you go, there you are.* Then she dropped a shoulder and used it to nudge her way through the packed crowd. Needing air. Breath. And time.

She really needed more time.

But all she got was, *No, no, no, no, no, no, no*, pounding in her head in time with the music. For this couldn't be happening. It wasn't possible that she, Charlotte Goode, wild child, rebel, hustler, lucky to pass English in school, thrower of cake, might actually have found her way to accomplishment in multiple areas of her life, all at one time.

Friendship, self-sufficiency, self-worth, respect in her chosen field.

With Beau Griffin the cherry on top.

No, he wasn't the cherry. He was the foundation beneath it all. For until *he'd* come on the scene, she'd been flailing. Barely holding it together. And now…now she was struggling to picture her life without him in it.

There she'd been thinking how great she was doing, how she was ready to launch herself onto the world, when it had been his influence all along.

Another pair of young women stepped in front of her, and she had to pull up so as not to knock them down.

"You're Anushka's maid of honour, right?" asked one.

"The fake one?" qualified the other.

The sharp tone had Charlie looking up. And while the hairs stood on the back of her neck, she was still on the job, still representing Anushka's interests, not her own.

"I'm Charlie Goode, Always the Bridesmaid."

"Told you, Mika," the first said smugly to the second.

"Heard you, Izzy. You were that wedding-ruiner, right?"

Charlie's mouth popped open, only to find she had no words. For what were words when the piano that had been dangling over your head, the one you'd spent months waiting to fall, clanged as it dropped to an inch above your head.

Izzy, hand on hip, said, "You drove the van carrying the wedding party into the lake."

"No, silly. She gave an entire wedding food poisoning."

Charlie wondered, for a blissful moment of freefall, if she might actually get out of this, when Izzy clicked her fingers. Pulled out her phone, scrolled a moment, then read, "Charlotte Hashtag Cakegate Goode ruins twelve-thousand-dollar dress in cake-tossing assault."

Then she held up her phone, assaulting Charlie with the zoomed-in image of herself, mouth agape, hand raised, crumbs falling from her tightly closed fist. And for a second she barely recognised herself. The foiled hair, the uptight clothes, and her eyes—they looked so tortured.

"We have to tell Anushka, right? What if she does something terrible? What if she ruins everything?"

Charlie excused herself and walked away.

What else could she do? No point in denying it. The cat was finally out of the bag. It was done. Telling them Anushka *knew* was putting Anushka in the middle of what was no doubt about to hit the fan.

There was also the fact that Charlie had felt a sudden overwhelming sense of *relief*.

For it turned out being found out was far less pressure than having so many things in her life going right at once that she didn't know where to turn.

Charlie was sitting on a pile of crates in an alcove outside the industrial kitchen when Beau found her.

"Hell, Charlie. Where have you been? I've been looking for you everywhere."

She looked up. Saw him walking toward her—tall, and beautiful, and draped in moonlight.

"Anushka?" she asked.

"Is just fine. She's saying her goodbyes before they head off. I told her you were putting out a literal fire with your bare hands and would be in touch when she got back from their honeymoon."

Charlie nodded.

"Are you okay? Did something happen? Can—?"

"I'm leaving," she said. "This week."

"To go where?"

"Edinburgh. First to visit my mum, then to find somewhere to settle."

"You mean you're *leaving* leaving? That soon? But what about the business? What about the house? The…the vegetable garden?"

"I've been clear from the start that that was my plan."

"But I thought—"

"You thought what? That I'd stay? Why? Did you think I was all hot air? Did you not believe I'd go? Did you not believe in me? God, it's the 'fixing my light' thing all over again!"

Beau flinched, as if she'd accused him of a great and terrible crime. Which, she knew, in his eyes she had. Because of all the people in all the world, Beau Griffin had always believed in her most of all.

More than she even believed in herself. But she was on the *right* path now, the path she'd decided on before he'd knocked on her door and upended everything, and this time she was not getting off.

"What happened between the dance and now?"

"What do you mean?"

"Charlie," he said, madder than she'd ever seen him. "Don't."

She deflated, looking down at her feet, her heels kicking against the bottom crate. "Some-one…confronted me. About #cakegate. They're in there now telling Anushka—"

"Who already knows and does not care."

"And likely telling anyone else who will listen. Meaning I can't go back in there. I'm done. It's *over*."

"Which, since you are apparently leaving this week, should not matter a jot."

Charlie pressed her lips together, realising no matter what she said, she would dig herself further and further into a hole. The only way out would be to tell him the truth—that she was falling for him and it was messing everything up.

Which wasn't his fault because look at him. It was all on her, because she knew better.

Beau watched her, waiting. Before he huffed out a breath and looked up at the sky. "I wondered what you might do, if something like this were to happen. I even thought you might react this way. That your instinct would be to run. I just… As we got to know one another again, I began to hope that that instinct might send you running to me."

Charlie breathed out hard. A war going on inside her. Team Charlie versus Team Beau. For that's what this felt like. As if she was fighting for her life.

"If you don't face this thing, head-on, own it, explain yourself or don't, but look it in the eye and let it go, it will consume you."

"Really?" she said. "This coming from the guy who, instead of facing his own grief, ran away to his childhood home and knocked the thing down."

Beau's jaw worked, his gaze glinting in the darkness. Then he said, "That's entirely fair."

Fair? That's not how this worked. He was supposed to fight back. To tell her she was wrong and he was right. Hell, she'd take one of his threatened pie charts or slideshows right now, so that she could throw her hand in the air and leave. Feeling vindicated that she had made the right choice.

For even while she stubbornly stuck by her plan, how did she know if it was right? It might end up being the absolute worst. All she had, all she could cling to, was that it was hers.

Beau looked back at her. "Do you *want* to leave?"

"I have to."

"I know you think that, but do you want to?"

"I don't see how that matters."

A beat, then, "It matters to me."

Charlie swallowed. Even her inner monologue was starting to panic, whispering, *Stick to the plan, stick to the plan*, over and over again.

When she said nothing more, he looked at the ground, and lifted a hand to the back of his neck, as he said, "I can't do this, Charlie. Strike that. I can. I did so, for years. What I *can't* do anymore is watch you do this to yourself."

"And what is it that I am doing to myself?" Charlie was very glad for the cloak of darkness, as she felt tears gathering at the corners of her eyes. For Beau was pulling away. Which was what she wanted. Didn't mean she had to like it.

"This," he said, waving a hand at her, before turning it on himself. "I thought it was just in you, that wild *stubborn* streak of yours that always sent you headlong into danger. Now, I wonder if it's deliberate. So that you have a ready excuse for any time things go wrong."

Charlie flinched, his words so close to the bruise in her core she gasped. "Beau?"

"And I get it," he said, pacing now. "I get why you did that. Your bastard of a father expended so much energy telling you how useless you were in the end it was easier to find ways to prove him right. But he was wrong about you, Charlie. For you are a strong, empathetic, ingenious, fiercely protective force to be reckoned with. And you never needed to prove that to anyone but yourself. But if you can't get over that, even now…"

Beau's gaze turned hard. His disappointment so keen Charlie felt it slice right through her. But she said nothing. She just looked at him as if what he was saying made no difference. When it made so much difference, he made so much difference, that it overwhelmed her.

As if he finally saw how fragile she felt, he let his hand drop and looked at her. "After Milly… Losing her like that, it was nearly too much for me. And you… You're… I can't keep worrying if you're going to climb a busted ladder in gum boots, Charlie. It hurts, like a fist in my chest, caring so much all the damn time."

Had he just said he cared so much for her it hurt?

While the thought wound around her heart,

again and again and again, Charlie said, "Then lucky for you we are on the same page."

At that a light went out in Beau. She saw it extinguish from his gaze, as if it had been a real thing. A thing she'd put there, that she had now taken away.

After a few long beats he nodded. Then nodded again. "Okay. Okay, then." Then, "Are you coming back in?"

She shook her head. "It wouldn't be fair to Anushka, not if people are talking about me. The best thing I can do, right now, is go. And since my time is up, consider yourself off the hook, too."

She'd tried to sound cavalier, to try to end this someplace that didn't feel as awful as she felt right now. But the way Beau looked at her, all rumpled and beautiful and stony, he knew what she really meant.

Not just that he was free to finish the gig, but that this was goodbye.

When one of the kitchen staff came outside, to toss a bag of scraps into the compost bin around the corner, he paused when he saw them, offered a quick smile, then went straight back inside.

Beau and Charlie looked at one another in silence, saying more by saying nothing than all their words had conveyed. This had been wonderful, life-changing in fact, but it had always been destined to end.

Charlie pressed herself off the crates, and walked

over to Beau. She placed a hand on his chest, and lifted herself to her toes to kiss him on the cheek.

Unlike every other time she'd done so, he didn't move a muscle.

"Thank you for your help," she managed. Then, "Good luck. With everything."

Then she walked away.

And while she got her wish, leaving him this time before he had the chance to leave her, the closure she'd thought it might bring was very much not there.

CHAPTER TWELVE

CHARLIE SAT IN the car in the driveway, revving herself up to bring in the fertilizer and packing boxes she'd picked up from Phil at the grocery store.

Instead she sat, listening to the Zombies play on the car radio, and looked at her front veranda. Funny that she thought of it as *her* front veranda now, right as she was getting ready to leave.

It did look nice, though. For she'd weeded the heck out of the thing one afternoon the week before, tearing out dead shrubs, trimming others, sweeping and hosing till it was tidy and inviting.

Then she checked her phone. Something she'd done a zillion times since the weekend. Waiting for some awful message from the Kents. Or a voice note from Julia, in case the news had hit her already.

The one person she was sure she'd not heard from was Beau. And at least there she'd been right. Turned out being right didn't feel as great as she'd always imagined it would.

And yet, when her phone rang, her first thought was, *Beau*?

It was, in fact, a video call from her mum. She quickly checked her face, in the hopes she didn't look as ragged as she felt, then answered.

"Hey, Mum," she said when her mother's face popped up. Her hair windswept, her skin a little burnt.

"Hey, honey."

"What's up? All good with you?"

"Great. Alfredo and I have taken up ocean running."

"It must be, what ten degrees, max?"

"Probably."

"Well, I'm not doing that."

Her mother laughed. "What's that I can see in the back seat there?"

Charlie lifted her pone. "Fertilizer."

"Are you making a bomb?"

"What? No!"

"Don't get so pernickety. I distinctly remember you coming home from the library with the ingredients to make a bomb one time. Poor Beau, the boy from next door, was standing behind you, shaking his head at me, a promise he'd never let it get that far."

Charlie's heart leaped into her throat.

"If not for a bomb," her mother said, "why do you need fertilizer?"

"For your old veggie garden that I replanted."

"Aren't you on your way here in a few short days? If so, who'll look after the veggie garden, then? Best to let it go, honey."

Charlie licked her lips. "Yeah, you're probably right. Thanks, Mum."

"Okay. Well keep me up to date with the packing. Talk soon."

When the screen went black, Charlie let her phone drop to her lap as she sank down deep into her seat.

Best let it go, honey, her mum had said, in that easy singsong way she had. Even after spending twenty odd years with her father, she was so chipper. So free. As if she'd woken up one day and let that go.

As easy as that.

Then she had Beau's voice in her head, telling her to face up to the choices she'd made. To own them. Maybe what she needed to get out of this funk was a mixture of both.

Own up, then let go.

And something that had been itching at the corner of her head the past few weeks stepped fully formed into her mind as if waiting for its moment.

#Cakegate Leesa had owned her own business, and according to Charlie's occasional Instagram stalking, still did. Before she could overthink it, she opened the notes app on her phone, copied the apology she had written, and edited, and polished a dozen times over the past two years, and this time sent the thing.

If she was going to own up to how she'd gotten to this point, she had to start there.

Next, she sent Anushka a message, reiterating how wonderful it had been to meet her, wishing she and Bobby a fantastic honeymoon and delightful life together.

That time her phone buzzed instantly.

Charlie Goode!!!

She'd have known those exclamation marks anywhere.

I'm so upset with you right now.

Charlie gulped.

A little bird told me you had a run in with a pair of nasty vipers at MY wedding. As of now, they know that if they breathe a word of the thing we will not name, I will be their mortal enemy. But when I get back, we are putting this nonsense to bed, once and for all. You and me babe. Besties forever.

Charlie's throat felt tight as a drum, when her phone buzzed again.

Dear Charlotte,

I was surprised to hear from you after such a long time, but I appreciate you reaching out.

Yes, it was a rough few months. For you, too, I saw. I am in a much better place now and I honestly hope that you are, too.

Richard and I are no longer together. In fact, we've not been together since the day after the wedding, when he explained how you knew one another. And I put two and two together as to the cake toss.

Did you know, he used me as a human shield? What a douche.

Regards,

Leesa

Her phone buzzed again. This time with a voice message from a call she must have missed while talking to her mum.

"Hey! My name is Cherry, I'm a friend of Anushka's. I was at the wedding and she raved about you. And I was hoping we could meet to see if I could take you on. It's a June wedding—"

Charlie turned her phone to silent and tossed it in the glove compartment, as if it were a live snake. For that was a lot to unpack.

The first on the list? Beau.

She'd always thought of herself as the carer of the pair, the one looking out for him. But if he'd been looking out for her, worrying about her, doing what he could to stop her from blowing the two of them up...even back then, it was a wonder he'd given her another chance at all.

Beau, who'd clearly been in touch with Anushka, letting her know what had happened so that she could leap into action. Working quietly behind the scenes. Making sure she had a support network to take care of her.

Beau, who'd not asked to be swept into her craziness, but once there, must have found he liked it. For he'd kept coming back for more.

Beau. The love of her damn life.

As soon as she thought the words, a rush of something wonderful flowed through her. Something bright, and sure, and true.

She loved him. She loved him so very much.

She loved that he was the listener to her chatter. The solid to her flux. The cool reason to her spit and fire. She loved that he was the arms around her, the whispers in her ear, the protective shoes to her dancing feet. She loved that he was her foundation, and loved that he rocked it, too.

Charlie loved Beau.

Only now that she'd owned it, she did *not* want to let it go.

"So, what now?" she asked out loud. Glancing to the tall shrubs blocking her view of the house next door.

Yes, loving Beau was terrifying. For she was as likely to get it wrong as she was to get it right.

But so long as she fixed it more times than she burned it down, it might actually all be okay.

Beau sat on the huge couch in the lounge room leading onto his balcony, big brown eyes looking up at him, a cool wet nose pressed into his palm.

For they had come to an understanding the past couple of days, he and Moose. Mike the electrician had dropped the dog off not long after he'd returned home from the wedding. Beau had stripped down and climbed in to bed, too spent, emotionally and physically, to clean himself up first. When Moose had nudged his way into Beau's bedroom, climbing onto the end of the bed, Beau had pretended not to notice.

A breeze swept into the room, through the concertinaed windows, bringing with it a "wet forest" scent with a hint of roses. And Beau breathed deep. Deeper than he'd have been able to only a few short weeks before.

Which, considering he'd spent the past few days feeling as if he'd been hit in the chest with a mallet, was saying something.

He remembered saying something as much to Charlie, during that wild conversation in the dark outside the kitchen. About feeling as if he had a fist in his chest all the time.

Because she made him worry.

Because she made him care.

Now, without the *boom-boom-boom* of the Spice Girls playing in the background, and the tightness in the back of his head after not being able to find her for a good half hour, and the scent of vegetable scraps in his nose—now that he had lost her—he was beginning to have a better idea of what that feeling truly was.

The reason Charlie made him feel as he was walking around with a fist in his chest was because he loved her.

He knew he loved her. He'd known it from nearly the first moment he'd seen her again. As if it had been inside him, waiting.

Only loving, for him, had always been tied up with loss. His parents. Milly. He'd already lost Charlie once.

He hadn't been in any place to foster those feelings, to nourish them. He'd wanted to break things, knock down his pain and build something over it to cover the scars.

But Charlie wasn't having it. She went about feeding him, distracting him, giving him projects and companionship, a safe space to heal, just as she always had. In doing so, she'd quietly kick-started his heart.

Given him perspective. Given him time. Eased his pain.

Even after the night of the wedding, her decision to leave, his to stay, it didn't feel quite the same. There was no emptiness, no rage. For his love for her remained. A solid visceral thing. As if it lived in him still, unchanged, never to be lost.

He looked up when a knock rattled his front door.

Likely someone selling energy plans, he thought. Or a kid playing ding-dong ditch.

Until the second louder knock roused Moose from his place at Beau's feet. His claws scrabbled on the polished floor as he bolted to the door. Then sat there, looking at the door, looking at Beau, looking at the door—

Knock. Knock-knock. Knock-knock-knock.

"Coming," he murmured.

Then, after patting Moose in that soft spot at the back of his head, he opened the door.

She was turned away, looking up, watching a flock of birds make patterns in the sky, but he'd have recognised the shape of her anywhere. The shaggy dark auburn hair, the curve of her neck, the fine points of her shoulders, raised slightly as if permanently ready to throw down.

"Charlie?" he said, his voice raw.

Charlie turned, sunlight blinding him a moment as it glinted off something she held in her hands. When it settled, and it was just her, standing before him. And the fist in his chest dissolved so that all remained was his heart, beating a steady tattoo for her.

"I wasn't sure you were going to answer," she

said reaching down to rub Moose's ear before the dog padded back inside, job done.

"Yet you kept knocking."

"I can be stubborn, don't you know."

Beau smiled, and leaned in the doorway, not about to make it easier for her. She'd threatened to leave him, after all.

"You could have come in the back way," he said.

"After the way I behaved?" She shook her head. "This felt like a 'formal entrance' kind of moment."

"This is a moment?"

She nodded. "I had hoped it might be. In fact, I have a whole plan to make it so. If that's okay with you?"

"Charlie," he said, his voice rough as hell. "I'm here. I'm listening. Just tell me what you came here to say. I want to hear. I'll always want to hear it."

The smile she gave him held literal hints of sunshine. He'd fight you on it.

"Then here goes. The other night, I freaked out."

"I am aware. I was there."

"Right," she said scrunching her eyes up tight. "So, you were. A lot of things all came at me at once that night. Hopes, dreams, feelings, beginnings, when I'd been so focused on the ending. This…thing I wanted so badly to do on my own."

"What thing?"

"Um, win at life?"

Beau laughed. "And what does that look like?"

"That's the thing. I thought I knew, but it turns out I did not. I saw a photo of myself just after I tossed the cake. Before that moment I'd thought I was on my way to winning life, but in the photo I looked as if, even before it was taken, I was already stressed, and unhappy, and not myself."

"Sounds like a lot."

"It was. None of which is an excuse. It's an explanation, I hope, as to why I behaved so unfairly toward you. When you were there doing me a favour."

She looked up at him, her gaze so heartfelt he wanted to wrap her up and make her feel warm, and safe, and loved. And it was clear she had more to say.

Which was: "If it's any consolation, I read somewhere that people often behave their worst around those they care about the most. Certain that person will love them no matter what."

"Is that right?" he said, holding onto the fact Charlie had just told him that he was the person she cared about the most. And that she knew he loved her.

That would make what he had to say much easier. Then again, a person would have to work awfully hard not to see that he adored her. And always had.

"I'm so sorry," she said.

"I know. And I'm sorry, too."

She shook her head. "What on earth do *you* have to be sorry for?"

"I'm sorry," he said, moving so he could join her on the porch, because now that she was there, she was still too far away. "For the time we missed that final year of school because I was too scared to tell you how I felt about you. I'm sorry I waited until the day before I left to tell you I was leaving, making you think I didn't worry about how it might affect you the entire time. I'm sorry I didn't tell you that even the possibility of a 'spin the bottle' game landing on you was the best moment of my life. Until that moment."

She blinked furiously, her cheeks pinking, her eyes now sparkling.

"You've had better moments since."

"I can think of a couple," he said, taking a step her way. He lifted his hand, cupping her cheek, gently. Feeling, deep in some entirely non-scientific place inside him, that this moment was the first of the rest of their lives.

And while he knew there would be disagreements, and risk, and that she'd freak again and again, there would also be star gazing, and laughter, and this love of theirs that had no regard for time.

When her eyes began to close, her mouth pop open, he said, "What have you got there?"

"Hmm?"

He glanced at the box she was holding, the one stopping him from being able to haul her into his arms.

"Oh, right. I... Well, I brought you a house-warming gift."

She held it a second, as if the way things had gone just now, she wasn't sure she needed it anymore. But Beau clicked his fingers till she handed it over.

He reached into the gift bag and pulled out a wooden sign. Twee and feminine, all curlicues and shabby chic paint, clearly custom-made from one of the artisans in Montville or Maleny. The letters *MWWF* had been etched into the front.

"*MWWF?*"

Charlie checked them, her mouth moving as she read, even though he knew she'd have checked them three times over. Then, looking up at him, one eye scrunched tight, she said, "It stands for Myrtle Way Weapons Facility."

Smiling, then laughing, loudly, at the awful audacity of the thing, Beau turned to hold it up against the sleek, eye-wateringly expensive reclaimed wood cladding, just above the minimalist. "Here do you think?"

"Gods, no." Charlie reached for it. But he held it out of reach. When she pressed up onto her toes and jumped for the thing, her body bumped against him.

Her eyes flew to his, and before she could slide

back to her heels, Beau dropped his face to meet hers. After a beat in which he made sure she knew what was coming, he pressed his lips to hers.

Her sigh was the most wonderful sound. The way she kissed him back, her lips clinging to his, pressed into every tender space inside him. Marking him, for life.

When he pulled back, she looked as dazed as he felt.

"I love it," he said. Then as if was the most natural thing in the world, "And I love you."

She blinked. Then demanded, "Say that again."

The hand not holding the sign slid around her back and drew her close. "I love you, Charlie. I love that you feel things deeply. I love that life was never able to smooth away your spikes. I love that despite the confidence hits you took as a kid, you made a career of making sure those under your charge never feel the same way."

"Beau," she said, reaching between them to grab great handfuls of his shirt, and give him a shake. Her eyes were diamond-bright, her face pure joy. And when she said, "I love you so much I can barely breathe right now," he felt it like an arrow straight to his heart.

"I love you," she said again. "I love you, I love you, I love you! I love you so much I feel like such a fool for not telling you the instant I knew. I love that you are so kind, and clever, and patient, and warm. I love how much you love my cooking, when the truth is I'm not all that great. I love how much you love your friends."

She stopped then, lifting a hand to her heart. For Milly. Who, in her own way, had brought them back together.

"I love how you listen. I love how you think. I love how hard you've worked to meet Moose halfway, and how much Matt's kids love you. I particularly love how much I love you."

Beau laughed. Then pulled her closer still. Into his arms, forever this time.

"Beau Griffin," she said, her eyes darkening, as she curled herself against him. "You really are the best man I've ever known."

Beau groaned. "You really went there?"

"How could I not? It was right there, waiting for its moment. And if we are doing this, for real, it's best you know what you're getting into. My penchant for puns. My heretofore unrevealed love of curing fish. My daily three in the morning trumpet practice—"

Before she could say another word, Beau scooped her up. She whooped, grabbing him around the neck. Then settled into his arms with a sigh.

"If we are doing this for real?" he repeated.

She lifted her face to kiss him. "Oh, we're doing this."

After which he carried her over the threshold, and into the first day of the rest of their lives.

EPILOGUE

CHARLIE AND BEAU sat on the balcony of their house on Myrtle Way, watching as the cockatoos took their twice daily commute overhead, stopping for a spell in the jacaranda at the rear of the yard, messing with the thing till a carpet of lavender flowers blanketed the grass beneath. Then they were off, following the last vestiges of the autumn sun.

The silvery light of the low-slung moon glinted off the ocean beyond, while the sky around them pinked, the smattering of cloud soaking up the last warmth before the sky seemed to pause, then darken on a single long outshot of breath.

Charlie leaned forward, or as much as she could, considering the size of her belly these days. To think their backyard had been piles of rubble, a danger zone Beau would have called it, his beautiful face so serious, a blink ago. Now it was a beautiful flat field of lush grass, set off by the retaining wall dripping in bougainvillea. Her series of raised veggie gardens stuck out like a sore thumb in the beautifully landscaped grounds, but Beau assured her it was his favourite part.

The fact that there was an actual fence now where the rose bushes had once been had been a…conversation. The symbolic thorny wall that had tried to keep them apart all these years was no more. Though they had replanted one of each variety in planters along the side of the house and walking past them, drinking in the nostalgia, was one of Charlie's favourite things.

A gate had been built into the fence at least, so when the house next door had finished with its refurbishment, and Matt and the kids moved in, they'd have easy access both ways.

Charlie shook her head, marvelling at how much her life had changed over the past year.

After Anushka had come home from her honeymoon, she'd taken Charlie by the ear and convinced to come on her radio show, and take part in a long-form interview about second chances. She'd given her side of #cakegate, talked about what she'd done to move past it, told of how she and Leesa had become Instagram friends, and how Always a Bridesmaid had sprung from the ashes. Thus turning what had been the defining moment in her life to a mere footnote.

Once Matt and the kids moved up, and with her mum and Alfredo coming over from Scotland for a prolonged visit when the baby was born, and with Julia the bookkeeper no longer a book-keeper, having bought into the business and taking admin and training, there was little time to ponder. To look back.

A good thing, though, as it turned out winning at life was really about living it.

"Moose!" she called, when the goofball of a dog sniffed at her baby carrots.

He looked around, wagging his tail, then bounded off down the hill.

Beau moved in behind her, gently moving to sit in a chair with him when he saw she was rubbing at her lower back. He lifted an arm and she leaned to rest into the curve of his big body. His other hand held the book he'd been reading. Some dense tome with more scientist terms than she cared to learn.

"What day are Matt and the kids getting here?" she asked.

"A week today, I think. He has a couple more things to iron out before, then LE goes into production, then they're on their way. If the house isn't ready, they can stay here?"

"Of course." When the kids arrived, the first thing she'd show them was how to sneak under the backstairs, where she'd already put a large metal chest that held a blanket, a torch, and a new pack of Uno cards.

Even after moving in with Beau, Charlie had

continued cleaning out the house next door. She'd taken classes on re-grouting a bathroom, and watched videos to learn how to pull up carpet. Someone had to teach their daughter how to do it.

Beau could teach her how to fix anything mechanical. How to be charming on the phone when you wanted something fixed, as Charlie didn't have the patience. He was like a bear with a sore head if she left him in his home office too long without dragging him out for food, or water, or fresh air, so he wasn't perfect.

But he was to her.

She'd known it the moment they'd met. When he'd stood at the bottom of the tree in his backyard and looked up and found her—crying, inconsolable, knees grazed, filled with anger at the things her father had just called her.

He'd said, "I'm Beau. Is it okay if I just sit here a while?"

And then he'd sat at the bottom of the tree, bending blades of grass into patterns, building forts for ants. There, in case she needed someone. In case she needed him.

"Are we ready, do you think?" she asked, placing her hand over Beau's.

"Probably not," he said easily, "but it's too late now."

True, she thought, snuggling into him with a happy sigh.

"You are going to be the most ridiculously gorgeous dad."

"While you will be the fiercest mum in living history."

"Unless, of course, you've made me too soft. Gooey. All blissed out."

Beau gave her a look that made it clear he believed her fierceness was there to stay, and that was fine with him.

Then, because she was done holding things back from this man of hers, she admitted, "I just hope that they'll be okay. That other kids are nice to them. And that they find that one great friend. And that they have my gumption, but your judgement. And—"

Beau moved, putting a halt to her stream of consciousness. He placed the bookmark in his book—no dog-earing for him, her beautiful rule-following man—and shifted till her eyes caught his.

Then, reaching for her chin, he stroked the sides of her face before leaning in and kissing her gently on the mouth. When he pulled back, he had the thrill of the fight, the fight for *her*, in his eyes, as he said, "You know what they will have? Guaranteed?"

"What's that?" she asked, so much hope filling her that she could barely contain it.

"They'll have us." With that, Beau kissed her again.

And Charlie knew, in her heart of hearts, that no matter what life threw at them from here, it was going to be more than okay. With this man by her side, it would be wondrous.

* * * * *

If you enjoyed this story,
check out these other great reads
from Ally Blake

Secretly Married to a Prince
Cinderella Assistant to Boss's Bride
Fake Engagement with the Billionaire
Whirlwind Fling to Baby Bombshell

All available now!

HARLEQUIN
Reader Service

Enjoyed your book?

Try the perfect subscription for Romance readers and get more great books like this delivered right to your door.

See why over 10+ million readers have tried Harlequin Reader Service.

Start with a Free Welcome Collection with free books and a gift—valued over $20.

Choose any series in print or ebook. See website for details and order today:

TryReaderService.com/subscriptions